# ROADKILL

## (BOOK 1)

## BY K.L. RAMSEY

Copyright © 2020 by K.L. Ramsey.
Cover design: Lee Ching with Under Cover Design

Imprint:Independently published

First Print Edition: May 2020
All rights reserved.

No part of this book may be reproduced, scanned, or distributed in any printed or electronic form without permission. Please do not participate in or encourage piracy of copyrighted materials in violation of the author's rights. Thank you for respecting the hard work of this author.

This is a work of fiction. Names, characters, places, and incidents either are the product of the author's imagination or are used fictitiously, and any resemblance to locales, events, business establishments, or actual persons—living or dead—is entirely coincidental.

## Table of Contents

| | |
|---|---|
| CILLIAN | 7 |
| VIVIAN | 13 |
| CILLIAN | 27 |
| VIVIAN | 36 |
| CILLIAN | 54 |
| VIVIAN | 63 |
| CILLIAN | 76 |
| VIVIAN | 92 |
| CILLIAN | 101 |
| VIVIAN | 110 |
| CILLIAN | 119 |
| VIVIAN | 132 |
| CILLIAN | 141 |
| VIVIAN | 167 |
| CILLIAN | 179 |
| VIVIAN | 187 |
| CILLIAN | 197 |
| VIVIAN | 206 |
| CILLIAN | 218 |

CAT 241
REPO 248

# PROLOGUE

# SAVAGE

Savage sat in the holding cell, waiting for the officers to bring Cillian in to see him. He knew his old friend would call him for help sooner or later. Cillian James was the one he failed and Savage lived with that disappointment in himself every damn day. Savage was good friends with Cillian's dad and had been since they arrived from Ireland when Cillian was just a kid. He promised to keep an eye on him after his parents went back to Ireland and Cillian stayed in the U.S., but somewhere along the line, Savage failed him.

When Cillian tried to join Savage's MC, he refused him. Patching in the kid would have been the wrong call. He didn't belong in that group of military misfits and one-percenters who made up his motley crew. To Savage, they were family but to Cillian, they would mean the end of what he wanted—a chance at a normal life. So, he told the kid that he didn't want him and even made up some excuse about him being too hot-tempered for their club, just to throw him off the scent. It had the opposite effect though and Cillian became even more determined to find his way in. Even if that meant joining Savage Hell's rival club—the Dragons. They were bad news and before Savage could step in and save Cillian, he had stolen a car to try to prove his worth to the Dragons. The problem was—they didn't want Cillian and when it came down to it, they let him rot in prison over a gang prank that went wrong.

Their leader thought it would be funny to set Cillian up to take the fall for grand theft auto and he took the bait and was now serving his time for the crime he committed. It pissed Savage off knowing that he could have prevented all of Cillian's problems if he had just let him into Savage Hell. But, it was too late to go back and change all of that. All Savage could do now was help his friend and he was hoping that was why he was summoned to the prison so early on a Monday morning.

The steel door creaked open and Cillian walked in wearing handcuffs and a smile. The officer instructed them that they were not allowed any physical contact, they only had ten minutes for their visit, and asked Savage if he wanted Cillian's cuffs on or off.

"Off," Savage growled. As soon as the handcuffs were removed, Cillian sat down on the other side of the table from Savage and nodded.

"Thanks for coming, man," Cillian said.

"No problem, Cillian. It's been a damn long time," Savage said. "I've been here a few times, but you refused to see me—what was up with that, man?"

Cillian chuckled and Savage sat back to cross his arms over his chest, finding the whole thing less funny than his friend.

"You haven't changed a bit," Cillian said and Savage just shrugged. "It's been a long time since I heard anyone call me by my real name. I was starting to forget who I was in here."

"Yeah, I heard about all of that," Savage said. "You got into some trouble. I heard you killed a man." Cillian eyed the guard who stood in the corner of the room, watching and listening to every word they were saying.

"Nope," he said. "But, I got the credit in the yard for it and that's how I got my nickname—Kill." Cillian flashed Savage a grin and he shook his head.

"It doesn't suit you," Savage growled. "I think I'll stick with your real name, Cillian." His friend didn't seem at all put off by him refusing to use his new nickname, even shrugging it off.

"Suit yourself," he said, his Irish accent sounded in full. Savage didn't realize just how much he had missed his friend until just now.

"It's good to see you," Savage whispered. "So much has happened since you've been in here."

"Yeah well, ten years is a damn long time. And, I'm sorry about turning you away when you came to visit but I just couldn't see you. Knowing you were here for me was enough but seeing you would have pained me. I would have longed for a life that I could never have." Cillian's expression was bitter and Savage realized that the boy he used to know wasn't sitting across the table from him. Cillian had become the man that prison had made him. He truly was 'Kill' now but Savage refused to believe he couldn't have the life he wanted, once he got out of that awful place.

"Why am I here now?" Savage asked, cutting straight to the chase. The guard was watching the clock and he knew that their ten minutes were just about up. It was time to find out why Cillian wanted to see him now after so much time had passed.

"I'm getting out," Cillian breathed.

"That's great, man," Savage said. "When?"

"Probably sometime next week. The date hasn't been set yet but my lawyer said it's a done deal. I need an advocate on the outside," Cillian all but whispered. "I was hoping it would be you."

"Of course, anything you need, man," Savage offered and he meant it too.

"I can't be around any felons, as part of my parole conditions," Cillian said. Savage nodded his understanding.

"So, no Savage Hell party at the clubhouse to welcome you home then?" Cillian smiled.

"No," he agreed. "I appreciate the club taking me under its wing after I did what I did with the Dragons. Savage Hell and you have had my back through all of this, but I can't be around most of the guys while I'm on parole."

Savage laughed, "Yeah, they aren't the upstanding citizens your parole officer will want you hanging around with, I'm afraid," he said. "But, you have my help—whatever you need."

"Can you pick me up and help me find a place to live and maybe a job, once I get sprung?" Cillian asked. He fidgeted with his own hands on the metal desk and for just a minute, Savage caught a glimpse of the shy boy who came from Ireland and didn't quite fit in anywhere.

"Of course," Savage said. "Consider it done."

"How's the family? I got your letters about Bowie and Dallas—I'm so happy for you, man," Cillian said. Savage wasn't sure if he believed him or not. He could hear the undertones of sadness in Cillian's voice.

"You'll get there too, Cillian. Someday—"

"Don't," Cillian barked. "Don't give me hope for someday, Savage. It hurts too much to think about not having that happiness in my life—a wife, kids—a family. It's not for me now so don't feed me some bullshit about someday," he growled. Savage nodded, knowing that now wasn't the time to argue with his friend. Not when their precious time was ticking down to mere seconds.

"That's time," the guard called. "Let's go, Kill." Cillian stood as ordered and nodded to Savage.

"I'll be here when you get out, Cillian," Savage promised.

"Thanks, man," Cillian said. The guard put the cuffs back on him and he turned to leave the room. "I knew I could count on you, Savage."

# CILLIAN

Kill had been counting down the days to his release and what was promised to be only one week away, ended up being two. When the day finally arrived for him to be released, Savage was waiting for him just outside the prison gates as promised. He was the one guy Kill could count on and he had to admit that it felt damn good to have someone on his side for a change.

During his exit interview with his parole officer, he was quickly reminded about the fact that most inmates end up right back in prison after they were let out. Kill didn't want to believe he could so easily end up as a statistic, but it was his biggest fear.

"Hey, man," Savage said, pulling him in for a quick hug. "You look good."

"Yeah, thanks for sending in some clothes for me. The ones they had of mine, from ten years ago, weren't exactly going to fit." Savage looked him up and down as if sizing him up. He was just a kid when he went to prison for grand theft auto—just twenty-three. It seemed like a lifetime ago.

"No," Savage said. "I guess they wouldn't. You have filled out in the last ten years."

Kill laughed, "Yep. Not much else to do in prison besides lift and workout."

"Well, I have a few bags of clothes in the trunk. Nothing fancy, just some stuff the guys got together and my girl loves to shop. Dallas had a field day picking you up some clothes. She even guessed your size and got you a suit, you know—for job interviews and stuff."

"I appreciate it, Savage. I'll find a way to pay you back," Kill promised.

Savage pointed his finger at Kill. "No, you won't. We're family and family takes care of each other," he said. "Now, get in. We need to get this apartment hunting underway. Until we can find you something, you'll be staying with me and my family. I've already given your parole officer my address and cell number." Savage got into the cab of his black pick-up and Kill slid into the passenger seat. He handed Kill a cell phone and he turned it over in his hand. He had never really had his cell phone and wasn't sure how to work the new ones. He only ever used the ones that flipped open but this one didn't have that feature.

"Push the side button and it turns on. It's charged and I've added you to my family plan," Savage said.

"This is too much, Savage," Kill whispered. It was too. He had forgotten what it meant to have family around and Savage treating him like a kid brother made him homesick for something that didn't exist anymore.

Kill's parents announced they were moving to the States when he was fourteen. Leaving Ireland felt like he was cutting off one of his appendages. He reluctantly agreed to follow them across the pond but Ireland was a part of him and he still longed to go back. But now, he had nothing and no one to go back to. His parents returned home, to Ireland just after he turned twenty-one, and he foolishly decided to stay in America. He was trying to get into Savage's MC—Savage Hell and he thought he was too good to go back to his childhood roots. He told his father that he wanted to stay in America and make something of himself, even implying his dad couldn't hack it in the States. God, he was an asshole. His father persuaded Savage to keep an eye on him and his parents headed back to Ireland.

About three months later, he got the call from his Mum that his father had died. He had a heart attack in his sleep and she found him dead the next morning. He didn't even go home for the funeral, even though his mother begged him to. Savage offered to lend him the money, but a mix of pride and being a stubborn ass took over and he refused. It was one of his major regrets and now that he was looking back, probably the one thing that shoved him down the wrong path. His life seemed to spiral out of control after his dad passed and one wrong decision led to the next and before he knew it, Kill was sitting behind the wheel of a stolen car, trying to prove he was worth something.

He begged Savage to let him into Savage Hell. Kill showed up to the bar that housed the club almost daily and every time Savage denied him; it drove him further over the line. When the Dragons showed interest in him, he jumped at the chance to be a part of a motorcycle club. He thought he'd show Savage just what he was made of by joining the Dragons and then he'd let him into Savage Hell. He was an idiot—he knew that now. But, at the time, it seemed like such a great plan. It wasn't and that point hit home when he realized his new club set him up. They knew he was mixed up with Savage and they used him to send Savage Hell a message. Dante was the president of the Dragons and he told Kill that if he wanted to be patched in, he needed to steal a car and bring it to the meeting. He wanted to be a part of something so badly he didn't think through the ramifications and getting caught seemed like a risk worth taking. He didn't even get a half a mile down the road with the car he stole before the cops pulled him over. During his hearing, it came out that he was set-up by the Dragons who were cooperating fully with the authorities. The judge decided to make an example out of him and gave Kill a twelve-year sentence, of which he served ten and with good behavior, got out.

About a year ago, he got a letter from his aunt in Ireland, telling him that his Mum had passed from cancer. He didn't even know she had the disease and it just about broke his heart that he didn't get to say goodbye to her. After his sentencing, she wrote him a letter, telling him that she would always love him, but that would be the last he'd ever hear from her and she was a woman who was true to her word.

"You good, Cillian?" Savage asked.

"Yeah," he lied. "Just thinking about everything. This is all a lot to take in," he admitted.

"Give it time, brother. You will have to do a lot of adjusting, but I believe in you, man. You need help, you use that to call me," Savage ordered, nodding to the cell phone Kill was clutching like it was his lifeline.

"Will do," Kill agreed. "And, thanks, Savage."

"Don't thank me yet, Cillian. You're bunking with the new baby and he'll keep you up all damn night long." Savage laughed.

"Remember, I've been in prison for the last ten years. Rooming with a newborn will be a piece of cake," Kill said.

"Yeah, we'll see if you're humming the same tune tomorrow morning when he wakes you up at four A.M., man," Savage said. "Welcome to the family, Cillian." Savage had no idea what those words meant to him and Cillian swallowed past the lump of emotion in his throat. It felt damn good to have a family again—now he just needed to find his place in the world—his home.

# VIVIAN

Vivian Ward wasn't sure how she was going to fit in everything on her to-do list today but she was determined to make that happen, even if it ended up killing her. The diner was once again short-handed, thanks to a teenage employee who thought it was all right to give all her friends free food. Viv knew her grandmother would have given the girl a second chance to, "Make things right," as she liked to say but that wasn't her style. Viv was hardcore when it came to giving people second chances, a life lesson she learned when she found her husband in bed with the town whore.

She had been married to Jason for almost three years when she came home early from her restaurant to surprise him. Truth was, she was the one surprised, finding him in bed with another woman. He made excuses and God help her, she was stupid and desperate enough to believe him. Hell, she even forgave him but that was just part of her need to be wanted and loved—well, according to her therapist. They had done the whole therapy thing and a year later, almost to the day, when she found her husband's secretary on her knees, under his desk giving him a blow job, she was done. Viv walked out of his office and went home to pack up his shit and kicked him the fuck out of her house. Honestly, it was the best decision she had ever made and she didn't regret leaving Jason even once. Sure, she was a little lonelier but she would rather be alone and happy then with a man she couldn't trust. Gone were the days when she'd sit at home and worry that her beloved husband was making bad decisions. Every time he couldn't account for his whereabouts, she'd go half-crazy and fly off the handle, only to let his soothing lies calm her. Yeah, she was a class A fool but not anymore. She was done with liars, done with cheaters and done with men in general. Lesson learned.

Today, she had bigger problems. She was down to just two employees and one of them was a new trainee. She was fucked until she could find another person to hire. Putting an ad in the paper and waiting for the right person to walk through the door took time—time she didn't have.

She blew into the diner like a tornado and found Tina going over how to refill the napkin holders with the new guy—who's name she could never remember—and Viv rolled her eyes. "You know Tina," she said seeming to startle them both, "I'm pretty sure that filling a napkin holder is self-explanatory." Tina nodded and handed the empty napkin holder and a stack of napkins to the trainee and bounced off into the kitchen. Viv suddenly felt way too old to be keeping company with the teens she usually hired. At twenty-eight, she should feel anything but old. But that was the problem with owning the town's only diner. Teens seemed to flock to the place in droves and they were also the ones who usually answered her ads for employment. Maybe if she held out this time, she'd find someone who could not only help wait tables but also have some experience behind the grills. Her current cook showed up to work on the days he was sober and those were becoming few and far between. She needed to get her grandmother's old place back on track and running as smoothly as it had when Gram was alive.

When Viv was seventeen, her Gram dropped the bomb that would forever change Viv's life—she had cancer and not much time left. Gram had raised Viv since her father took off and her mother died. She was only six years old when the two most important people in her life abandoned her but Gram stuck around. It took time to realized that her grandmother wasn't going anywhere and when Gram announced that she had terminal cancer, it hit Viv hard. She promised her Gram that she would take care of her beloved diner but that was easier said than done. Her grandmother fought hard but when Viv was twenty, she passed, leaving her to take care of everything—alone. She had never felt so lonely, not even after divorcing Jason. Her grandmother was her everything. Maybe that was why she was willing to overlook all of Jason's flaws and accept his marriage proposal. Viv believed that being with someone—anyone—was better than being alone. But boy, was she wrong.

Luckily for her, Gram had taught Viv the ropes at a very young age. She had been helping in the diner her whole life and taking over ownership of the place wasn't a stretch for her. Her grandmother had thought of everything and arranged for her lawyers to handle the transfer upon her death. Viv showed up to work the day after the funeral and opened the doors for business, much as she always had. It's what her grandmother wanted and she honored her wishes. Gram insisted that she get on with her life as quickly as possible and Viv promised to try. Throwing herself back into her work seemed as good a way as any to get on with life.

"Hey, new guy," she shouted. The trainee turned from trying to shove way too many napkins into the holder and pointed to himself as if to ask, "Me?". Viv sighed and nodded. "Do you see any other new guys around?" she asked. Sure, she sounded like a class A bitch but she didn't care.

"N-no," he stuttered.

"You wait tables on your own yet?" she asked but Viv already knew the answer by his blank stare. "All right then," she said under her breath. "Today you learn to wait tables on your own. It's sink or swim time, New Guy," she said.

"Um, my name is Tommy," he nervously offered.

"Of course it is," she whispered to herself. "Okay, Tommy," she said, turning to hand him an order pad and pencil. "You write everything down. If someone says to hold the onions, write the letter O down next to the order and then cross it out," she said. Tommy nodded and started jotting down notes as she went over everything and she couldn't help her smile at remembering the way Gram used to ride her for not using the correct codes for the kitchen.

Viv had taken to abbreviating everything and when her order went back to the cook, he had no freaking idea what the hell to make of it. Gram told her to get it straight or she'd have to deal with the pissed off kitchen staff. After she was yelled at a few times by the cook, Viv learned quickly to avoid his temper and write the correct fucking codes down on her order pad.

"Get the codes right or deal with the cook," she barked at Tommy. He nodded and started to write down her orders, word for word and she sighed again. "This is going to be a long fucking day," she breathed.

Viv busied herself getting the diner ready to open and didn't even see the wall of man that she ran into while making her way to the back storeroom. "What the fuck?" Viv growled, taking a step back to get her bearings. The guy's big, tattoo-covered hands quickly reached out to her, helping her to find her balance.

"Who are you and how the fuck did you get in here before we're open?" Viv asked. She looked him up and down and realized that most of his exposed skin was covered in ink and she had to admit, it was hot. She had always liked bad boys even if she had married a clean-cut accountant the first time around. Her grandmother used to say, "If he rides a motorcycle or has tattoos, my granddaughter will date him." She wondered what her Gram would think of the sexy man standing in front of her now. His light brown hair was long and wavy, hanging down to his broad shoulders. Honestly, he had better hair than she did and she was suddenly regretting her decision to go a third day without washing it, opting for a messy bun. He looked like he worked out but not the way the muscle heads at the gym did. This guy looked more naturally fit but his muscles seemed to have muscles. His amused smirk told her he wasn't buying her tough girl routine either.

"I'm here for breakfast," he said and his voice sounded like a warm brandy coating her soul.

"You're not from around here, are you?" Viv asked.

He chuckled, "Nope," he said. "Although I call the fair state of Alabama my home now, I'm originally from Ireland."

Dear Lord, Viv felt about ready to burst into flames just from his sexy voice alone. His accent made it harder for her to concentrate on what her next question or comment should be. Hell, she was pretty sure that remembering her name might be a task.

"Can I get some food?" he asked when she didn't respond.

"Food?" she repeated as though she didn't understand the word.

"Sure—you know, stuff you eat. Listen, I have a busy day and I just need to fuel up." Viv looked down at her watch and back up at the sexy, tatted man before her. He took off his black leather jacket and flung it over his shoulder, giving her a better look at not only his tattoos but his muscles. And, holy arm porn—he was hot!

"Fine," she said, trying for a little pissed off but sounding a whole lot more turned on. Shit!

"I'll just sit here at the counter if that works," he offered. She didn't say a word, not sure that anything she uttered would make any sense. Viv just stood there nodding like a fool and watched as he walked past her to find a stool at the front counter. She nearly swallowed her tongue at how good his ass looked in the black jeans that hugged him like a glove. She shook her head as if trying to regain her senses.

"New guy," she barked. "You're up."

"Tommy," he called from the corner of the diner. "My name is Tommy," he complained.

"Yeah, yeah. Tommy—you're up," Viv corrected and didn't miss the way hot biker guy laughed.

"Keep laughing," she warned. "Tommy here is in training and you're his first real customer," she said not hiding her smile. "Good luck to you, Sir," she said and turned to finish her work in the back storeroom. She needed to take a quick inventory for the day, especially since her now ex-employee fed her friends as though it was her personal pantry. She'd call in her order and then find the time to post a new ad in the local paper.

By the time she finished her inventory, New Guy had not only brought Hot Irish Guy his food but they were chatting it up like they were old friends. "Don't you have something you could be doing?" Viv looked Tommy up and down and took a sadistic pleasure in the way he hopped out of her way and pretended to be busy.

"Sure, boss," he said. Viv pulled the sugar shakers from the counter underneath the bar and started to refill them. "Oh, Tina said to tell you she had to leave for the day. Something about a family emergency," Tommy said. He shot her a look that suggested he should be afraid to deliver the message and New Guy was right. She felt about ready to lob a sugar shaker at his head but that would only involve paperwork and workman's comp. claims she didn't have time for.

"Great," she mumbled. "That girl has more family emergencies that anyone else I've ever met. Just how big is her family anyway?" Viv complained to herself.

Hot Irish guy seemed to find her whole monologue funny. "So, you're employees giving you trouble?" he questioned. He shoved four pieces of bacon and half a piece of toast into his mouth.

"Trouble doesn't begin to describe what they are causing me today—or any other day, for that matter," she admitted. "I just fired Tina's best friend for feeding half the town for free and now she takes off with her same old tired excuse. It's just me and the New Kid," she said, nodding to where Tommy was still fumbling with the napkin dispensers.

Hot Irish guy cleared his throat, "I might be able to help with your troubles," he said. God, Viv thought of about a thousand ways that man could help with her problems and not one of them involved what he was probably about to propose. "Hire me," he said, holding his arms wide as if he was making a sacrifice to her.

"What are your qualifications, Hot Irish Guy?" she asked.

"Hot Irish Guy?" he questioned her nickname for him. Honestly, she was awful at names, so she usually made up her own for people.

Viv shrugged, "Well, it's accurate," she said. She put down the sugar shaker she was working on and studied him. "Really, why would you want to work here? I usually get high schoolers coming in here to ask me for a job, but you look to be well out of the public school system."

He threw back his head and barked out his laugh and it was probably the sexiest thing Viv had ever seen in her life. "Yeah, I'm well past school age, Darlin'," he admitted. "I'm just turned thirty-three." Now it was Viv's turn to laugh. He sounded as though he was saying "tirty-tree".

"Yeah, yeah—go ahead and may fun of the way I say my th's; everyone does." He shot her a sexy smirk that had Viv immediately stop laughing. This guy seemed to be able to take the whole smolder thing to a whole new level.

"My question stands," she said. "Why do you want to work here?"

He shrugged and pushed his empty plate to the back of the counter, leaning forward as if he was about to share a secret with her. Viv did the same, eager to share the same space as the sexy guy. "I'm a felon," he loudly whispered.

She didn't even blink an eye. She had known a few ex-cons in her life. Her grandmother even dated one for a few years until he got bored and took off. So, Hot Irish Guy's grand admission didn't shock her. "And incapable of whispering," Viv teased.

"You don't seem surprised." He sounded almost disappointed in the fact that he didn't surprise her.

"Let's just say that my grandmother sometimes ran with a questionable crowd and I've known all kinds," she said. "So you want a job here because you're a felon? You look other places?" Viv knew she was sticking her nose into a stranger's business but she couldn't help herself. Plus, if he wanted her to consider him for employment, she had a right to ask questions. Although, she was pretty sure that the question she wanted to ask was completely inappropriate. His relationship status didn't factor into whether she would hire him or not.

"Yeah," he admitted. "I've put into just about every place on Main Street who's hiring and nothing. I have to fill out their applications and when I get to the part where I have to answer 'yes' for convicted of a felony, it's over. No one wants to hire an ex-con." Viv hated that he seemed almost defeated and whether right or wrong, she wanted to help him.

"What did you do?" she asked.

"Grand theft auto," he answered. "I was a stupid kid—just trying to get into a motorcycle gang. My family had just gone back to Ireland and left me in America and I didn't exactly fit in." Viv giggled at the thought of an Irish kid trying to fit in with the kids around town. Kids in their little Alabama town were tough when it came to accepting anyone new into the fold. Given the fact that he sounded so different from them, Hot Irish Guy might have never found his place.

"I got about eight hundred meters before the cops caught up to me. I found out later that the guys in the gang I was trying to join set me up. I was made an example of by the system and served ten years of a twelve-year sentence."

"Wow, that's awful," Viv said and she meant it. What happened to him sucked and not giving him a chance to turn himself around would be a dishonor to her Gram. He was just the type of person her grandmother was constantly trying to help. And, now it was Viv's turn to lend a hand. Of course, it didn't hurt that Hot Irish Guy was—well, hot.

"I have two questions," Viv said.

"Shoot," he said, leaning back in his stool.

"Can you cook and when can you start?" His smile almost lit up the place and she knew she did the right thing even if New Kid was shooting her daggers from the back of the diner.

"What's the problem, New Kid?" she asked.

"He's not going to outrank me, right?" he asked.

"I don't think that's even possible, New Kid," Viv said, rolling her eyes for good measure. "Now back to work and stop eavesdropping." She watched as Tommy pretended to wipe down the booth he had been working on for the past ten minutes.

"How about we take this to my office and you can fill out the paperwork?" Hot Irish Guy nodded and grabbed his dishes.

"Thank you," he said, following her back through the kitchen to deposit his dishes into the sink. He followed her back to her tiny office and crammed into her space, making it feel even smaller.

"Um—" she squeaked, suddenly feeling nervous. "I guess you should tell me your name—unless you're good with Hot Irish Guy."

He chuckled and his deep baritone laugh filled her office. "It's Cillian James but everyone calls me Kill," he said.

"Kill?" Viv questioned. "That's a pretty ominous name. You have anything else you need to tell me before we make this official?" She asked.

"Nope," he said, taking the papers from her. "I'm good."

# CILLIAN

Kill watched the sexy little brunette fidget around her office as if she was too afraid to leave him alone in her space. He didn't blame her. There were a lot of people who didn't trust him and he'd just add her onto that very long list.

He finished filling out the paperwork and realized he didn't know his new boss' name. "Sorry," he said, startling her from her work. "I don't know your name."

"I'm Vivian Ward," she offered. "Usually, the kids who work for me just call me boss but you can call me Viv." He stood and held out his hand and she hesitantly took it.

"It's good to meet you, Viv," he said. "You won't be sorry you gave me a chance here."

"I don't know." Kill worried that she had already changed her mind and he set the papers down on her desk. "With a nickname like 'Kill', I think I might have bitten off more than I can chew." The thought of his hot new boss biting anywhere on his body flashed through his mind. He needed to remind his unruly cock that wasn't going to happen—not with her now that he was her employee. At least, he hoped he was still employed.

"Listen, if you're having second thoughts, I understand," he lied. He didn't understand any of what he had been put through this past week since getting out of prison. He had been treated like shit and all he was asking for was a chance to prove that he wasn't that same stupid kid who desperately wanted to be a part of something.

"How about you tell me how you got your nickname and I'll reserve my final decision until you are done sharing your story?" He hated having to recap any of his time in prison but if that was the only way he was going to get a job, he'd do it. Still, it felt wrong telling someone who seemed as innocent as Vivian Ward about something so personal and dirty from his past.

"I got it from my cellmate, in prison," he whispered. "I was thrown into general population and I had to survive."

Viv gasped and covered her mouth with her shaking hand. He almost regretted telling her anything. "And you had to kill someone to stay alive?" she guessed.

"Yes and no," he admitted. "I didn't kill anyone but everyone believed that I had, so I let them think the worst of me."

"Why would you let them believe you killed a man?" Viv asked. He didn't expect her to understand. Prison changed a person and when you were in there, you learned to do whatever it took to make it out alive.

"We were in the yard—you know having some free time and I was approached by a man they called Capone who was in charge, so to speak, of the prisoners. He had ties to the mafia and was from a rival club on the outside. Even though I had been thrown in prison before becoming a member of the Dragons, he considered me an enemy."

"Why didn't you tell anyone?" she asked. He chuckled at the idea of telling someone what was going on in that yard. Hell, he'd be labeled a snitch and they got a hell of a lot more than stitches in that prison. They ended up in the infirmary if they were lucky and in the morgue if they weren't.

"Who was I to tell? If I reported every illegal activity going on in that place to the warden, I'd end up in the morgue. I tried to talk to some of the gang members—you know the ones who set me up? Like my new friend, Capone, they didn't consider me to be a part of their club. They had heard what happened to me on the outside and told me I was on my own."

"What happened next?" Viv asked. She sat in front of him, on the edge of her desk and it took all his restraint not to reach out and pull her onto his lap. Feck, she was sexy and he was going to have to work damn hard to remind himself that she was off-limits. He had to admit the way she seemed to take an interest in him turned him inside out. It had been over ten years since he was with a woman. Hell, he'd been out for a week and the first thing he wanted to do was find a willing woman and spend a night losing himself in her, but he didn't. That would have been his way of falling back into his old habits and he couldn't let that happen. It was the strait and narrow for him and that meant no gangs, no drugs, and no hookers, no matter how much his dick screamed for attention.

"When Capone heard that I was on my own, left for dead by my own supposed club, he did something that completely surprised me—asked me to join his prison club. I had nothing to lose and everything to gain by taking him up on his offer. When the rival gang came after him for taking me in, a guy got killed. Capone was the one who shanked him but gave me the credit. He knew that with a rumor like that going around, that I killed a guy, I'd be safe while serving my time. Capone took the blame and had time added onto his sentence and I got the nickname 'Kill'," he said.

"Wow," she breathed.

Wow is an understatement," he admitted. "Hell, if I hadn't taken his offer, I'd be dead now. He taught me the ropes and kept me safe," Kill said. He thought about his friend still sitting in that prison and felt an unexplainable sadness that he had gotten out.

"Aw—a bad guy with a heart of gold," Viv said, interrupting his thoughts.

"Yeah, you could say that about a lot of the guys on the inside. I know this might sound crazy but I'm going to miss that camaraderie," he admitted. As soon as he got out, he met with his probation officer who informed him that meeting with any type of club or gang would land him back in prison and he would do anything not to have that happen.

"Why can't you join a club out here?" Viv asked.

"It goes against my parole. It would be considered a violation since trying to join a motorcycle club was what landed me behind bars, to begin with," he said.

"Oh, I'm sorry." She reached out and placed her small hand over his forearm and his skin felt strange—almost like pins and needles. Yeah, he was going to have to find a woman and let off some steam if just a simple touch from his new boss set his skin tingling.

He pulled his arm free from her hand and pretended to stretch to cover his retreat. "No," he said. "It's just a part of what I have to do to stay on the outside— you know, find a job and a place to live and keep my nose clean."

"How long have you been out?" she asked.

"About a week," he whispered.

"Do you have everything you need?" Viv looked him up and down and damn if she didn't look just as turned on as he felt. She cleared her throat, "I mean, did you find a place to live and all that?"

"I'm working on the job part first and staying in a motel that's a shit hole, but the owner lets me rent by the week. I figure getting a job trumps a place to live if I can't pay the rent. My friend said I could bunk at his place but he's got a family and a new kid. The last thing he needed was an ex-con hanging around. After a few nights with his family, I felt like a nuisance. I made some apologies and came up with an excuse as to why I had to leave. It was just too much for me—going from a small prison cell with one roommate to a house full of people. I think Savage understood. At least, I hope he's not pissed that I turned down his generosity and opted for my shithole apartment."

Viv nodded. "You have a friend named Savage?" she asked.

Kill smiled at the fact that little piece of information was her takeaway. "Yeah," he breathed.

"Well, um—you have a job," she said. "As long as you're okay with me calling you by your given name, Cillian. And if you need a better place to stay, I have a house about a block away. It was my grandmother's." She paused, "All of this was hers and she left it to me."

"I'm fine with you calling me whatever you'd like. Hot Irish Guy, Kill or Cillian—as long as I have a job," he said. "And, I'm sorry about your grandmother. Losing family sucks," Kill said.

"It's fine. She's been gone awhile now but I think she would have liked you. She always routed for an underdog and you seem to be as down on your luck as they come. How about you move into my spare room? We can work out the details of pay and I can take your rent out of that." He wasn't sure what to make of her kind offer. On the one hand, he needed a place to stay long term and he had to admit that any place had to be better than the motel he was currently in. But, his gut was telling him that living under the same roof as his sexy new boss was a giant mistake. The last time his gut screamed at him that way was the night he decided to do the stupidest thing in his life and steal a car.

He ignored his gut and nodded. "Thanks, Viv," he said. "I'll take you up on your offer of the room and I can start now if you need." He pointed back to where he remembered the kitchen to be located.

"Great," she said. "You never answered my other question, you know."

He thought back over their conversation, trying to pinpoint which question she was talking about. "Oh?"

"Yeah, the one about you having any cooking experience," she reminded.

"It just so happens that you're in luck, Darlin'," he said. "I was put on kitchen duty while in the clink and I learned from the best fry cook you'll ever meet." Viv's smile brightened up her tiny office.

"Perfect," she beamed. "Let's get you started." She stood and led the way out of her office and all Kill seemed capable of doing was watching her sexy little ass sashay out. Yeah—he should have listened to his gut when it came to his hot as fuck new boss. He was a glutton for a punishment and Kill was pretty sure that having to live under the same roof as Viv, and keeping his hands to himself, was going to be a pretty big fucking punishment to endure.

# VIVIAN

Viv wasn't sure what the hell had gotten into her, inviting Cillian to move into her spare bedroom wasn't her finest decision. Now, she was going to have to spend every waking moment in a state of perpetual horniness and that was going to be her stupid fault.

Hearing his story and seeing the sadness in his eyes, just about broke her heart. There was no way that she'd let him walk out of that diner tonight knowing that he was heading back to the shitty motel he was staying in. It wasn't who her grandmother had raised her to be. And who was she kidding, it helped that she was completely taken in by his bad-boy charm and the sexy Irish biker thing he had going on.

The diner hummed to life before lunchtime, just as it usually did every day. She catered more to the lunch crowd and didn't mind. In the evening, she got a lot of little league teams coming in for ice cream and snow cones. That was the best thing about living in the South, there was never a downtime for her business. When her

Gram started the diner, it was just an ice cream parlor. Her grandmother spent some time up north one summer and fell in love with snow cones and came home to add them to the menu. After a while, people from town started coming in and asking if Gram had a lunch menu and the concept of the diner was born. Her grandmother poured her life savings into turning what was a simple place to get an ice cream cone into a full-fledge diner. They had their loyal customers and business never seemed to fall away.

Viv couldn't remember a time when she didn't want to run the diner. When she was little, her Gram told her that she should go to college and she could be whatever she chose to be but Viv would insist that she wanted to own the diner someday. When her dreams became a reality, she realized that owning a restaurant wasn't as easy as her Gram made it look. The hours were grueling and didn't leave much time for friends or dating, for that matter. She had a few steady boyfriends over the years but no one stuck. When she couldn't give them what they seemed to want—her time, they took off. The only guy who stuck around was her ex-husband, Jason. Viv had a feeling that her grueling hours spent at the diner allowed her unfaithful husband to pursue other women around town. She was a fool and played right into his hands, but that was all in the past.

The entire day seemed to zip by and she spent it waiting tables with the New Kid and keeping a close eye on Cillian, making sure both were learning the ropes. She had to admit that Cillian seemed to know his way around a kitchen and everyone raved about his chili during the lunch rush. She was sure that hiring him had been a good call but the rest of it—the part where she asked him to move into her house and rent her spare room, felt like the worst idea of her life. Still, she wasn't a chicken and she wouldn't back down from her offer. She had already made it and there would be no going back now. That didn't mean she wasn't going to be responsible and make sure that there were some rules in place to keep her personal life private from her professional life. Viv needed to remember that Cillian James was a part of her professional life—period.

"Ready to head out?" she asked, turning the corner into the kitchen. "Wow—I don't think I've ever seen this place cleaner," she said. Cillian looked up from where he was washing the last big pot and smiled but she noticed it didn't touch his eyes. Maybe a twelve-hour shift was too much for his first day. She suddenly felt bad for not giving him more breaks and reading the signs she was pushing her new employee too hard.

"You look tired," she said.

"Thanks," he grouched. "I'm just not used to a full day's work. We usually had to work a four-hour shift since they didn't want to let us out of our cages for too long unless it was necessary."

Viv wasn't quite sure what to say. "Well, good news—it's quitting time. We can head home and you can get settled."

Cillian loaded the clean pot on top of the pile of others and wiped down the sink. She wasn't sure he was going to say anything so she turned to head back to her office to grab her things. She shut down her laptop and packed her bag, shutting off the lights and closing her door, to walk straight into a wall of muscles and tats—Cillian.

"Woah—" he grunted, his arms banding around her middle to help steady her.

"You keep doing that," she complained. "You need a bell around your neck or something to warn others that you're on the move," she teased. Cillian laughed and she realized that he still had his arms around her waist. She looked down at them and back up at him, trying her best to cock her eyebrow.

"You okay?" he asked. "Your face is doing something weird."

"I'm fine," she said, swatting his arms away from her. So much for her subtle hints about him touching her. She was just going to have to come right out and say what she was thinking.

"Listen," she started.

"Shit, I've been out of the whole scene for a while, but if I remember correctly when a woman starts her sentence with 'listen', things get ugly," Cillian said. "We have a problem here?" he asked.

Viv wanted to insist they didn't but they did—a huge problem. "I'm not sure if you're aware of this or not but you're a nice-looking guy," she said. God, her heart was beating like a teenage girl and she was sure the next time she opened her mouth, she was going to vomit.

Cillian puffed out his chest and stood a little taller and Viv could feel her eyes roll. "Thanks," he said.

"Okay, now you're just being ridiculous," she said. "I was going to try to make this less uncomfortable for both of us but I'll just lay it all out there. We need ground rules." She felt as if she was holding her breath, waiting for Cillian to start laughing or make fun of her, but he didn't. Instead, he nodded his agreement.

"Wait—you don't think I'm crazy for wanting rules for us to co-exist under the same roof?" she questioned.

"Nope," he said. "I think it's a perfect idea. I mean you and I don't know each other and as you've pointed out—I'm attractive." He paused to bob his eyebrows at her and she giggled. "And you're sexy as hell—so I'd say ground rules are in order."

"Wait," she whispered. Her brain was backtracking, trying to grasp what he had just said. If Viv wasn't mistaken, he had just called her sexy as hell. "What did you just call me?"

Cillian tapped his finger to his chin as if he was thinking hard about something and she felt about ready to slap him. "I believe I called you 'sexy as hell'." He winked at her and took her bag. "So, these ground rules," he prompted. "Want to tell me about them on the drive home?"

"No," she protested, although just what she was saying no to was beyond her. Viv felt all turned around and completely off her game around Hot Irish Guy and it was starting to piss her off. "Yes," she growled.

Cillian had the nerve to chuckle as he held the front door open for her. "Which is it?" he asked. "Yes or no?"

"Yes, I want to go over ground rules but no, I didn't drive here. I told you my house was just up one block, right?" He nodded. "Well, I walk here most days," she said. "We can go over the rules on our walk home and then you can pack your stuff at the motel and move it over. I can give you a hand if you need." The only thing Viv wanted to do with the rest of her night was to take a hot shower and crawl into bed, but she was willing to help Cillian out to get him settled.

"No need to help," he said. "Everything I own fits inside of a small duffle bag." Viv locked the front door to the diner and was once again at a loss for what to say.

"Sorry," she said.

"For what?" he questioned.

"For everything," she said. "I seem to be saying all the wrong things since we've met. Truth is, I couldn't even begin to fathom what you have been through and I'm not sure what the protocol is for polite conversation around you."

"I'm not a polite conversation kind of guy, if you haven't noticed, Boss," he said. "I mean, I'm your employee now and I just told you that you're hot." He was right, she was blowing things way out of proportion, just as she always had and she was possibly going to scare off one of the best cooks the diner ever had.

"I'm sorry. It's just been a long day and I need about two days' sleep to get caught up. I promise I'm not this shifty," she said.

"So rules—what's the first one?" Cillian asked as if getting them back on track.

"Well, you are welcome to use the entire house and you'll have your room but we are going to need to share a bathroom. So, I think we should work out some sort of schedule?" she offered.

"As in I'll need to plan for when I will need to use the facilities?" Cillian teased. "I've been well trained—prison will do that to a guy, but I can't time that stuff."

"No," she said. "I meant for showers."

"Thank God, because if I have to guess every time I'm going to have to take a piss, I'd need to hire a psychic. Okay, so no fortune teller needed and rule one works for me. I can take a shower around your schedule, it's not a big deal. I hope to join a gym and might even shower there, just to help out with water and such."

"Are you usually this considerate?" Viv asked.

"No," he admitted. "I've been told I'm a class A asshole, but I'm in your debt for giving me not only a job but a place to stay."

"You don't owe me anything," she said. "I'm happy to help and with the way my customers loved your food today, I think I should be the one thanking you. I don't know what I would have done today if you hadn't come along. I probably would have had to shut the diner down until I could find help."

"Let's just call it a draw. It was a win-win for both of us," Cillian said. They turned the corner and when she got to the front of her house, she suddenly worried if he was going to like it as if that mattered.

"So, this is me," she whispered. "Well, I guess I should say 'us'."

"It's so nice," he said. "You said it was your grandmother's?"

"Yep, and I moved in after my mom died and my dad took off," she said. She had never told anyone else that part about her life. "Sorry, that was too much information."

"Listen, we're going to be living in the same house and we'll need to know things about each other. I've already told you just about all there is to know about me," Cillian admitted. Somehow, Viv didn't quite believe him. She was betting that he hadn't even scraped the surface.

"How about you go and grab your stuff and I'll make us something to eat. Will it take you long?" Viv asked.

"No," he said. "As I said earlier, I don't have much." She nodded and unlocked her front door.

"I'll have a key made for you tomorrow. Let me give you a quick tour and then you can get settled." Viv led the way into the kitchen and took her bag from him, noting the way his eyes flared when her fingers brushed over his hand. "This is the kitchen and if you go through that door, it leads to the family room and then the back yard. Upstairs, there are three bedrooms and of course, the shared bathroom I told you about. Feel free to pick which one of the spare rooms you want. They are both pretty much the same—bed, dresser, closet—you get the idea. It's not much but it's mine."

"It's pretty fantastic," he breathed. "When you come from having nothing, living in a place like this is almost a dream come true. Thanks, Viv." He paused in front of her and was so close she thought for just a minute he was going to kiss her. But, when Cillian took a step back giving her some space, she felt almost let down.

"No problem, Cillian." she turned to open the refrigerator, trying to find anything else to do rather than staring at the sexy man filling most of her kitchen. Having a roommate was going to take some time to get used to. Having Hot Irish Guy as a roommate was going to take every damn ounce of her willpower and then some.

---

Cillian took about an hour to run back to his motel and pack his stuff and when he pulled up outside her house on his Harley, she nearly swallowed her tongue. She had a weakness for men on motorcycles and her grandmother was right, she liked a bad boy. Cillian James seemed to be as bad as they ran—well almost. He was also the sweetest man she had ever talked to, although she was pretty sure he'd bulk at that description of himself.

Viv watched as he parked his bike in her driveway and when he started for the house, she ducked out of the front window and ran back to the kitchen and even banged some pots around, for good measure.

"Hey," he interrupted, dropping his bag onto the corner chair. "It smells great in here," he said.

"It's just some baked chicken." She shrugged, looking at his bag that held everything he owned. "You weren't kidding about not having much," she said nodding to his bag.

"Yep, I travel light," he teased. "What can I do to help?" Cillian took the plates from her and set them on the table.

"Grab the silverware and the bottle of wine from the fridge," she ordered.

"You have any beer?" He asked. "I'm not much of a wine drinker. Hell, I'm not much of a drinker at all. They don't serve alcohol in prison, you know."

"There might be a few in the back from—" she was about to say from her last boyfriend, but that didn't seem appropriate conversation between an employee and employer. This was new territory for her and she wasn't sure what to say or do.

"Your boyfriend?" he asked.

"He used to be. We broke up about three months ago and I think he left some in the fridge," she said. He rummaged through the top of the refrigerator and pulled three beers out and grinned over at her, making Viv giggle from the goofy triumphant look on his face.

"Found them," he said. He set everything down on the table and rummaged through her cabinets looking for a glass. Viv handed him her wine glass and finished putting the food on the table. "So, you want to go over the rest of the rules?" he asked. "I've got the first memorized," he teased.

"Shower schedule," she said.

"Yep," he agreed, pointing to his forehead, his long dark hair framing his beautiful face. "It's in the vault," he said. "What's the next one?"

"How about we let each other know if we will be entertaining," she said, using air quotes to frame the word "entertaining". "I don't mind you bringing a woman back here but I ask that you don't have an endless parade of them trudging through the house."

"Endless parade of women, hmm." He stroked his beard as if he was envisioning all of those women and she giggled.

"Okay Casanova," she said. "You get my meaning though, right?"

"Sure, no three or more-somes—got it." He smiled and winked at her and Viv shoved a bite of chicken into her mouth to keep from groaning at the idea of Cillian bringing a woman back to the house. He was a grown man who most likely felt like he had some time to make up for with the female race, but she didn't want to have to bear witness to the whole thing. She wanted to volunteer to help him blow off some much-needed steam but that would be foolish. It had been months since she had sex with someone or something besides her vibrator and breaking her dry spell with an employee was a horrible idea.

"Rule three," she said, clearing her throat to continue. "I'm not a maid or a chef," she said.

"I don't know Viv," Cillian spoke up. "This chicken is pretty fantastic."

"Well, thanks for that, but I don't want to have to clean up after you more than you probably don't want to do so after me," she said.

"Right—don't be a slob or a douche," he said.

"Are you taking any of this seriously? I feel that you aren't." Viv looked him over, hoping for stern but knowing she fell short by his amused expression.

"Sure," he said. Cillian reached across the table and took her hand into his. "I take the fact that I was a stranger to you this morning when you literally bumped into me and gave me a job—very seriously. You've given me a place to stay and that is also something I take seriously. Joking around is my way of hiding my emotions. Maybe I should have shared that earlier—it's one of my many flaws."

"You must be a hoot at funerals then," she teased. He rubbed his thumb over her hand.

"I've only been to one and I was a mess. I couldn't stop laughing and everyone thought there was something wrong with me." Viv had only attended two funerals herself. She thought back to her mom's funeral and how awful it was. She thought she would never feel so much sadness but she was wrong. Losing her grandmother nearly did her completely in.

"Were you close to the person?" Viv asked.

"He was a friend and it was a long time ago—when I was practically a boy back in Ireland," Cillian admitted.

"Your parents are still alive, then?" Viv prodded. She knew she was possibly sticking her nose in where it didn't belong. She justified her inquisition by remembering that she was effectively Cillian's landlord and had a right to know at least something about him.

"No," he whispered. Cillian pushed his half-empty plate back from where he sat and Viv felt like an ass for prying into his personal life.

"Sorry," she said. "Forget I even asked."

Cillian shrugged. "It's fine. My parents went back to Ireland when I was in my early twenties. They were only in America for about seven years and they missed home so much, my dad decided to move back. I thought I was big shit and when he begged me to go home with them, I refused. If I had just agreed, my life would have turned out so differently."

"How?" Viv asked. She leaned forward, resting her elbows on the kitchen table, fixated on the beautiful man sitting next to her.

"Well, as I said, I thought I was the shit. My father asked his friend, Savage, to keep an eye on me but I was quite the handful. I tried to join Savage's motorcycle club and when he turned me down, I looked elsewhere for acceptance. Let's just say that was the beginning of the end."

"I'm sorry," Viv whispered.

"You have nothing to be sorry about. It was all my doing. My dad died shortly after he got back home— heart attack. I was a stubborn ass and refused to go to Ireland for the funeral. Me not showing up broke my mother's heart and sent me into a downward spiral. One bad decision led to another and before I knew it, I ended up in prison. I found out my Ma died a few years later from cancer. I didn't even know she was sick."

Viv couldn't help herself. She slid her chair closer to Cillian's, resting her hand on his forearm. She wanted to give him comfort but wasn't sure just how far he'd let her go. "I'm so sorry, Cillian," she whispered.

"My mom died when I was a little girl and my dad couldn't seem to get a handle on life after her death. He took off and my Gram finished raising me. I know what it feels like to lose people you love but I can't imagine what it must have been like for you having to go through all of that from prison."

"Again, ending up behind bars was my own making," Cillian said.

"It still sucks," she admitted. "But, that's the thing with life," she said. "You can second guess it all you want but you can't go back and change the past."

"No, you can't," he agreed. "How about you, Viv? You have anything you second guess and like another chance at?"

That was something she never let herself do—wonder about what-ifs. Her life hadn't turned out so bad but she did see it going in another direction. Maybe one that involved a husband and kids but she still had time for all of that.

"Not really," she admitted. "I'm pretty happy."

"You wouldn't change anything?" he asked.

"Um, well, I'd like to get married someday and have a couple of kids," she said. Viv had never told anyone else that.

"That sounds nice," he said. "When I was doing my time, I never allowed myself to hope for things like that."

"And now?" Viv asked.

"Now that I'm out, I've started giving it some thought. I'd like a few kids but settling down right now seems like a pipe dream. Not many women out there can overlook my record." Cillian pulled his arm from under her hand and slid his plate back in front of him, taking a bite of his food.

"I have," she almost whispered. "Looked past your record, that is." Her voice was so quiet, she wondered if he had heard her but his stunned expression and nod let her know he had.

# CILLIAN

"Thanks for that," he said. "Not many people can see through all this." Kill held his hands out, gifting her with a view of his tats that ran up his arms. He knew what he looked like and he made no apologies for his tough outer appearance. It was who he was.

"How far up do your tattoos go?" she asked. Viv was staring at the ink on his arms and he decided to figure out just how much she'd want to see. Kill pulled his shirt over his head and he had to admit he felt a smug satisfaction at the way she looked his upper body over.

"Wow," she mouthed. He had most of his upper body covered in tats and if he dared remove his pants, which he figured would be a bad idea, she'd find a few on his legs too. "That's a lot," she said. "How did you get all these?"

Kill looked down his body at the road map of tattoos that told his life story. He remembered every single tat and the story behind each one. "I had most of them before I went to prison but got a few while I did my time," he said.

"You can get a tattoo in prison? Do they let you go to a tattoo parlor or something?" He didn't want to laugh at Viv's question, but he couldn't help it. She was so naive it was almost funny. He had never met someone quite like her before.

"No." Kill chuckled. "They don't give us day passes to go to the local tattoo parlor. Guys were crafty and sneaky and made their homemade machines. Some were good and some were shit, but it was just a part of it— you know the life. We paid in cigarettes and gum and stuff, to have them done. This one here," he pointed to a picture of his mother that had been inked onto his chest, just above his heart. "This is a picture of my mum." Viv leaned into his personal space to study his tat. She was so close to him; he could feel her warm breath on his bare skin and goosebumps rose on his flesh.

"You're cold," she said. He felt like his skin was on fire and if Viv knew that, she'd be backing away from him as quickly as possible. Ten years was a damn long time to go without having a woman and Viv was his wet dream. She was turning him inside out with need but Kill knew to keep that bit of information to himself or risk being tossed out on his ass.

"No—just the opposite. I feel as though I'm burning up," he admitted.

"O—Oh," she stuttered. Viv must have realized his meaning because she slid back from him as he slipped his shirt back over his head.

"Let me help you clean up and then I think I'm going to hit the hay," he said. Kill carried his plate over to the kitchen sink and started running warm water in, searching for the dish soap.

"No, you must be exhausted," she said. "Go on up and pick a room and get settled. Feel free to use the shower first and I'll clean up down here."

"Are you sure?" Kill asked. "You realized that you just ordered me to break two of our new rules," he reminded.

"Two?" Viv questioned.

"Yep. Rule one—shower schedule and rule three—you aren't a maid. Well, technically you've broken rule three twice tonight because you made dinner. So, you've been a chef and a maid, going against everything rule three stands for," he said.

"I guess the rules will just have to start tomorrow," she said.

"Really?" he asked. "You know, we never discussed a big rule—possibly the biggest rule between us." Kill was thinking about the fact that Viv hadn't specifically said that she was off-limits. Rule two was about parading women through the house but nothing about the one woman his whole body seemed to hum to life for. The one woman who seemed to make everything possible for him again. The woman who looked past his time in prison and gave him a chance—Viv.

She put the dirty dishes into the soapy water and turned to face him. "I thought we were pretty thorough and whatever we forgot, we can just add it later or wing it." God, he hoped she meant it because what he was about to do was going to be either epic or he was going to go down in flames. Either way, he had to take the chance.

"Alright," he said. Kill crossed her tiny kitchen and pulled her body against his own and his cock instantly sprang to life. Viv felt good—so good that he was willing to risk it all—his new job and a place to live, for what he wanted from her next.

"Cillian," she chided, swatting at his chest but he didn't budge. "What are you doing?"

"If you tell me no, this all stops here. I need to know something," he whispered. Viv stilled against his body and if he wasn't too off his game, she even leaned into him some, as if in invitation.

"What do you need to know?" she whispered back. Her full lips were mere inches from his own and it was taking all his restraint not to just take what he wanted without her permission. That wasn't who he was anymore—it didn't matter how long it had been since he was with a woman.

"I need to know if you taste as good as you look, Darlin'," he said. "Tell me no, Viv and this stops now," he reminded.

"What if I don't want you to stop, Cillian?" she asked. "What if I agree?"

"Don't tease me, Viv," he growled. "It's been a damn long time since I've been with a woman."

Her soft breath hitched and he could tell that she was just as turned on by the whole scene as he was. Viv still hadn't given him the green light and he wouldn't make a move on her without her consent.

"How long, Cillian?" she asked. "Since you've been with a woman."

"Just over ten years," he admitted.

"No special woman visiting you while you were away?" she asked.

"Nope," he admitted.

"You've been out for a week now," she said. He knew she was fishing but she wasn't going to catch anything.

He wondered who had hurt Viv that she had such trust issues, but that would be a question for another time.

"A week is hardly enough time to meet a woman and a prostitute just doesn't appeal to me," he admitted.

"Yes," Viv breathed and wrapped her arms around his waist.

"Yes, what?" he questioned, trying to keep up with their conversation through his haze of lust.

"Yes to whatever you want," she whispered. Viv leaned against him and gently brushed his lips with her own. Her's were so soft and when she gently tugged on his beard and demanded he open for her, he groaned into her mouth. He had forgotten just how soft a woman felt pressed up against his body, or how good they smelled and tasted.

Kill pressed her up against her counter and she straddled her legs around his waist. He couldn't help himself, he thrust his cock against her belly and she hissed out her breath. "You feel so fecking good, Darlin'," he growled.

"You do too," Viv said. "This might be the worst idea I've ever had but I'm not sure I care." Kill stopped kissing her and lowered her to the ground, taking a step back from her body. "What the hell?" she questioned.

"I don't want to be your worst idea," he said. "We can't do this if you feel it's a mistake," he said. "I won't be anyone's mistake."

"That's not what I meant, Cillian," she said. "You aren't a mistake and I would never think that. You are my employee and what if things don't work out between us? I have a diner to think of."

"I get it," he said, even though he didn't. His cock was protesting that he had stepped away from the soft, willing woman and he had to admit, he agreed. "What if we made a pact?" he offered. Kill was always good at thinking on his feet. It's what kept him alive all those years behind bars.

"What kind of pact?" she asked, crossing her arms over her impressive cleavage. Kill had to will himself not to look her body over.

"We agree that at work, everything remains strictly professional. You're my boss and I'm your employee," Kill began. "But when we get here, we are just two people who are attracted to each other, doing our thing."

Viv's smile nearly lit up the kitchen. "Doing our thing? What things would we be doing?"

"Um, you know—things. Like what we were just doing," he said. It had been so long since he was with a woman, he almost felt shy talking about sex. Hell, he was never shy when it came to women or talking dirty to them. He had lost his virginity at age fourteen when he convinced one of the town's girls to "see him off properly" before he headed to America. He used that line quite a few times to get laid before he and his family headed to their new home. Girls seemed to eat up the fact that they'd know someone in America but he never wrote or called any of them, as he had promised. He never talked to any of them again.

Once he got to America, his sex life was even better. American females seemed to love his accent and he learned how to lay it on thick when he needed to. He used his accent and his looks to his advantage. Getting women to agree to fall into bed with him was just one of the perks of picking up and moving with his family. It made having to start life all over in a foreign land a little easier and a whole hell of a lot more fun. He needed to remember his game or he was going to have to watch the sexiest woman he'd seen in a very long time, walk away.

"You know you can say sex," Viv teased. "We are two adults and I'm pretty sure neither of us is a virgin."

"Right," he agreed. "So, what do you say—a pact then?" He held out his hand for her agreement and she smiled and took it, giving him a yank into her body and wrapping her arms back around his waist.

"If I remember correctly, we were about here," she said.

Kill nodded and pushed her back up against the counter so she could straddle him again. "I think this feels about right," he teased. He wasn't sure how they would make any of this work but he'd worry about all the logistics later. Right now, all he wanted to do was sink balls deep into Viv's sexy body and make her yell out his name as many times as humanly possible.

Yeah—he'd worry about the rest tomorrow.

# VIVIAN

"Bedroom?" Cillian said between kisses. He had stripped her down to her bra and panties and she said a silent prayer that she was wearing a good set and not one of the ones that made her look like an escaped lunatic.

"Up the stairs to the right," she said. Her body felt about ready to burst into flames. She was consumed with raw need and passion she hadn't felt in some time. Viv was completely wrapped around his body, straddling his impressive erection as Cillian effortlessly lifted her into his arms. He carried her up the stairs and pushed his way into her messy bedroom.

"I wasn't expecting company," she said, suddenly distracted by her mess. "I don't usually do things like this—you know sleep with men I just met."

"God, I hope not," Cillian said. He was kissing his way down the column of her neck, nibbling and sucking as he went, and she was pretty sure she'd be wearing his mark in the morning. "I don't give a feck about your room or how tidy it is," he growled. "I just want you naked and underneath my body."

Well, that was something she could get on board with. Viv tried to block out the rest of the world and not think about her unkempt room or the fact that she was about to give her body to a man she had only met hours before—a man who was her new employee. She'd worry about all those things in the morning. Now, she just wanted to feel alive for the first time in forever and Cillian certainly did that for her.

He unhooked her bra and hissed out his breath, "Perfect," he murmured against her sensitive flesh. He sucked one of her taut nipples into his mouth and she felt a new pool of wetness between her legs. Viv ran her fingers through his long hair, grabbing handfuls of it to tug. He seemed to like it a little rough and Viv was fine with giving him what he wanted.

"I need you inside of me," she ordered. Cillian gave her a sexy, wicked smile and dared to wink at her.

"On the bed," he commanded. Viv did as he asked, loving the little power struggle they had going on between the two of them. It was seriously hot. Usually, men cowered and caved to her dominating nature but Cillian gave it right back to her. He hovered over her body and hooked his thumbs into the sides of her lace panties, slowly sliding them down her legs.

"Now you," she said, eyeing his boxers.

"Give me just a minute," he demanded. Cillian stood over her, looking her over like she was his next meal, causing her body to squirm with need. "Hold still, Viv," he ordered.

She stilled and smiled up at him. "Like this?" He nodded and finished his perusal of her naked body. When she started to worry that he had changed his mind about wanting her, he pulled down his boxers and stood gloriously naked in front of her. His erection jutted out towards her and she sat up a little to give his body the same attention he had just given hers.

When Cillian made a move to get onto the bed with her, Viv held up her hand to stop him. "Give me a minute," she said, giving him back his words. She looked him up and down, letting her eyes rest on his rather impressive erection. He palmed his cock, stroking his shaft and she nearly lost her mind. Viv was consumed with lust and all she wanted was to feel him pumping deep inside her body.

Finally, when she couldn't take any more of his teasing, she went up on her knees and reached for him. "Please, Cillian," she whispered. "I need you." He didn't seem to need any further invitation, climbing onto her bed. He lowered her back down to the mattress, covering her body with his own. He kissed his way into her mouth, and just when she thought she couldn't take waiting any longer, he thrust into her core without any further warning. She moaned at the sensation of being filled by him, thrusting her hips to meet his, trying to take more of him.

"God," he whispered. "You feel so fecking good, honey." Viv reached up to frame his beautiful face with her hands, loving the tender way he closed his eyes and leaned into her touch.

"You do too, Cillian," she said.

"It makes me so hot when you say my name," he admitted. "No one has called me by my real name in so long."

Viv smiled up at him, "Cillian," she whispered. He moaned, pulling his cock almost completely free from her pussy and slamming back in. "Cillian," she said. Viv leaned into his body, gently kissing his lips, loving the way he pumped in and out of her core. He took what he needed from her and gave her exactly what she wanted. It was almost as if he could read her mind and knew what she needed. When Viv was on the edge, ready to fall, Cillian reached his big hand between their bodies, running the pad of his thumb over her clit until she felt as though she was flying. She fell and he was right there to catch her.

He pumped in and out of her body with a new fury and when he came, it was her name he whispered over and over again until he collapsed on top of her limp body. "That was—" Viv wasn't quite sure how to finish her sentence. She wanted to say wonderful but that sounded so cheesy. She tried to think of another adjective that could completely describe what had just happened between the two of them but she was at a loss.

"Please tell me that was okay," Cillian begged. He was lying next to her, watching her as if his entire existence depended on her answer and she couldn't help her giggle.

"It was so much better than okay," she admitted.

"Thank God," he breathed. "I was afraid I was so out of touch, I'd forgotten how to fuck," he said.

"No." Viv turned to her side, wrapping her leg over his. "You didn't forget how to fuck, Cillian. I'm betting that time only made you better at it."

He nodded and smiled, "Well, when you have nothing else to think about while sitting in prison, you tend to compile quite a playlist of sexy scenes in your imagination. I can't tell you how many times I thought about meeting someone like you and doing this while I was sat there, waiting."

Viv couldn't imagine. Even when she was between boyfriends, she at least had her trusty vibrator to get her through. "It must have been very lonely for you," she whispered and cuddled into his side.

"Yeah, but it was what I had to do. I did the crime and even though they made an example of me and gave me extra time, I felt as though I deserved it. Prison saved me in a lot of ways," he said.

"How so?" Viv asked. She was past the point of worrying that she sounded too nosey with all her questions, now that they had fallen into bed together.

"It took me away from a life that was wrong for me. I was trying to join a club whose members didn't care about me or my well-being. I would have ended up dead or worse, in prison for murder if I hadn't gotten away from them. The guys from Savage Hell had my back while I was away. They're a club who cared about me and not just what I could do for them. They are my brothers —all of them. Not just the ones still back in that place but the ones on the outside."

"But, you can't hang out with them because it violates your parole," she reminded.

"Yeah," he said. "I have two years of parole and if I behave, I'll be able to do what I want. Not being able to hang out at my club is turning out to be harder than I thought it would be."

"So, you can't even talk to them—it's an all or nothing deal?" Viv asked.

"Yes and no," Cillian said. "I can't be seen in church or with any of the guys who've served time."

"Church?" she asked.

"It's what we call our meeting place—biker's church." Cillian's smile was sad and Viv wished there was something more she could do to help him out.

"Why not just hang out with the ones who haven't been to prison?" she questioned.

Cillian barked out his laugh, "Honey— we are a club of one-percenters and military misfits," he said as if she would know exactly what he meant.

"I have no clue what that means, Cillian."

"It means that most of the guys in my club are felons and have done some time on the inside. There is one guy—Savage, he's our leader. He's never been to prison so he's on my approved list of people I can see. He's the one who met me the day I got out and took me back to stay with his family. When I told him I needed to be on my own, he was the one who found me that shitty motel to rent. He was trying to help me find a job but he's got a lot going on himself. He's one of my best friends and more than that—he's my brother."

"Well, this Savage guy sounds pretty awesome," she said. "To help you out like that. I'd like to meet him sometime."

Cillian shrugged. "Sure," he said. "He and his husband and wife don't live far from here. Maybe we could all get together sometime. But, for now—" Cillian rolled her on top of his body, causing her to squeal. "How about we find some other way to distract ourselves?" Cillian swatted her ass and she smiled down at him.

"I like the way you think," she teased, grinding her pussy against his already erect cock. "You're ready again?" she questioned.

"I have a lot of time to make up for, Honey. You up for that?" Viv pretended to consider his request and he swatted her ass again, this time making her yelp.

"Yes," she hissed.

"Good," he grunted and pulled her down to kiss him. It was going to be a hell of a lot of fun helping Cillian to make up for lost time.

Viv spent the night tangled up with Cillian's demanding needs and by the time the sun had come up, she had barely slept a wink. She carefully extracted herself from Cillian's big body and pulled on his t-shirt. She padded down to the kitchen to find last night's dinner dishes still piled in the sink. She started the coffee pot and pulled on her dish gloves, refilling the sink with hot, soapy water. Someone pounded on her front door, scaring the life out of her. She dropped one of her dinner plates into the sink and it broke.

"Just fucking perfect," she complained. She took off her rubber gloves and walked down the hallway to the front door, grumbling to herself the whole way. She didn't bother to check out the peephole and threw open the door to find a man standing on the other side.

He began to speak and she held up her hand, effectively stopping him. "Listen, I haven't even had my coffee this morning, I've had a very long night and your pounding on my door at the butt crack of dawn caused me to break one of my favorite plates. So, this better be good," she growled.

The well-dressed man opened his mouth to speak again and Viv once again stopped him. "And, before you tell me you're here to sell me something, help me find Jesus or that I've won some sweepstakes I haven't entered, let me remind you that I haven't had my coffee yet and most days, it's the only thing that keeps me from killing people. Especially people who show up on my doorstep unannounced and pound on my door before seven in the morning. Now—" she said, taking a deep breath. "What can I do for you?"

He hesitated as if he wasn't quite sure she was going to let him speak at all and she wildly waved her hands in the air as if silently telling him to get on with it. "I'm looking for Cillian James. He also goes by Kill," he said. "I was told he works for your diner, Miss Ward, and I'm hoping you can tell me where I can reach him. His last place of residence called to tell me that he checked out last night and I'm worried he's in violation of his parole."

Now it was Viv's turn not to talk. She worried that she had just opened her front door and invited in trouble for the man who had spent most of the night making her his. The same man who was asleep in her bed.

"And you are?" she asked.

He held out his hand, "Jackson Hart," he offered as if that would explain everything. "But, everyone calls me Hart. I'm Cillian's parole officer."

"Oh," she breathed. Viv noticed the way he looked her up and down and suddenly realized she was wearing nothing but Cillian's Harley shirt.

"Hey babe," Cillian said, bouncing down her stairs in just his boxer briefs. "What's all the commotion?" He stopped dead when he found his parole officer at her front door.

"Hart," Cillian said. "Why the hell are you here?" he asked. Cillian looked Viv up and down. "Where the feck are your clothes, Viv?" he growled. Cillian moved to stand between her and his grumpy looking parole officer as if the damage hadn't already been done.

"He's already seen me," she said.

"Well, he's finished looking," Cillian growled. "You haven't said why you are here. I'm not supposed to check in for three more days."

"You checked out of your motel and they called to let me know," Hart said. "It's protocol."

"Bullshit," Cillian growled. "You're keeping tabs on me but you will find that I've done nothing wrong—so check away. I left my shit hole motel because I found a job and another place to stay. If you need me, I'll be right here."

"You didn't mention that you had a girlfriend on the outside." Hart almost sounded as if he was accusing Cillian of something and Viv could feel the tension rolling off his big body.

"I just met Viv yesterday. I will be working at her diner," Cillian said.

Hart tried to look around Cillian to where she stood in the doorway, but he blocked the parole officer's view with his big body. "You do know that he is a felon, right Miss Ward? I took the liberty to run your background check and you're clean—squeaky clean. Why would you associate with a known felon?" Now it was Viv's turn to be pissed. She sidestepped Cillian and stood almost chest to chest with his parole officer.

"You had no right to run my background check," she growled. "Furthermore, it's none of your fucking business what is happening between Cillian and me. I knew who he was when I hired him."

"And, how about when you fell into bed with him—did you know who he was then?" Hart asked. She could tell he was trying to make Cillian angry but why? He was certainly taking the bait. He was crowding the parole officer and she thought for sure Cillian was going to hit him.

"He's not worth it," she said, trying to get him to stand down. "Let's just go inside and have breakfast. You have Cillian's new address, Mr. Hart. I'd appreciate a heads up if you plan on stopping by my residence and for the love of God, come during normal business hours and not before I've had my coffee."

"I'll have my eye on you, James," Hart called after him as she tried to drag Cillian into her house.

"Good to know," Cillian called back over his shoulder, just before he slammed the front door in Hart's face.

# CILLIAN

A few months had passed and Kill had spent most of his days working at the diner and his nights in Viv's bed. Once he had her there was no way he was going to go sleep in the spare room. She didn't seem to protest his proposal when he said he'd like to share her room. They had become pretty much inseparable and Viv even ended up going with him to meet with his probation officer every week. He had a feeling that after her first encounter with Hart, she wanted to prove that she wasn't just some quick fuck. Not that Kill would ever consider her that.

Everything seemed to be working out for him until a few of his club buddies showed up at the diner asking to see him. Viv warned them that he'd be violating his parole if he agreed to talk to them but judging from the looks on their faces, something was up and he couldn't just turn them away. She agreed to let them use her office and when he asked her to give them a minute, he didn't miss the hurt and upset in her eyes.

"Fine," she scoffed. "But much longer than that and I'm coming back here to break this little meeting up."

"Deal," he agreed. He waited for Viv to leave before shutting her office door. "Let's have it, boys," he said. "You three don't look very happy to see me," he teased.

"It's Savage, Kill," Ryder said. Out of all the three of them, Kill knew Ryder the best. Repo seemed pretty cool but Snake had quite the reputation for being a badass. He was warned by a few guys in the group to steer clear of him.

"What's up with Savage?" Kill asked. Savage lived with his husband, Bowie, and his wife, Dallas, about twenty minutes from Viv's place. He hadn't seen much of them since moving into Viv's house and that was on him. Savage was one of his best friends. He helped him so much once he got out, even giving him some cash to get by until he could find a job. He had gotten caught up with his new life and woman, which was no excuse. Kill suddenly felt like a first-class ass for not checking in with Savage after everything he had done for him.

"It's his oldest kid," Repo said. "She's missing and he said to tell you he's calling in that favor you owe him."

"Chloe's missing?" Kill said. She was one of the coolest kids he'd ever met. She was only seven years old but she was as bossy as the day was long. When Savage took him apartment hunting, she liked to point out where he should put furniture and how to set things up. When Kill told her he didn't have anything to put anywhere, she quickly added that he should go out and buy some furniture. He told her he'd get right on that but everything changed so quickly for him.

"Tell me what I can do," he breathed.

"You aren't going to like it," Snake said.

"Just tell me what Savage needs me to do and don't worry about what I like and don't like," he said. "He helped me out when I got out and he's right—I owe him big time."

"He needs you to reach out to your contacts in the Dragons. He thinks they are the ones who took his daughter and he wants her back. Hell Kill, Savage will start a war if he needs to but none of us want that. You know that Savage Hell isn't the kind of club to go out looking for trouble. But, the Dragons took this on when they took Chloe," Ryder said. "Savage, Bowie, and Dallas are going out of their fucking minds not knowing where their daughter is."

"I bet," Kill said. "I'll reach out today to see if I can find out what's going on. My contact in that club is usually in the know. If Chloe's with them, he'll know it." Kill heard Viv's door creek open and knew that she had probably heard everything they were just discussing. He turned to find her very pissed off, standing in the doorway and his suspicions were instantly confirmed. His woman wasn't going to like the fact that he was taking off to talk to his old club but what choice did he have—it was for Savage.

"Thanks for letting me know, guys," he said, effectively ending their little meeting. "I'll be in touch as soon as I know more." The three guys filed out of the small office, each nodding politely to Viv except Snake who gave more of an inappropriate stare. Kill cleared his throat and Snake quickly found his way out of the office.

"You want to tell me that I didn't hear you right?" Viv asked. He wasn't sure what the right answer was, so he went with complete honesty.

"I'm a little out of practice here, baby," he admitted. "When it comes to women and what I'm supposed to say and not say—well, I have no clue. I'll just give it to you straight," he said.

"Yeah, that'll work," she sassed, putting both hands on her hips. He had never seen Viv so pissed off before and he had to admit it was pretty damn cute and even made him hot.

"Savage has a kid and the Dragons have taken her. Or, at least that's what Savage believes," Kill said. "I have connections to that club still and he wants me to make a few calls, to see what I can find out."

"Oh God," she said. "That's awful. Has he called the police?" Kill barked out his laugh and Viv looked him up and down as if he had lost his mind.

"Honey, the police don't get called in for shit like this. Clubs learn to settle the score in their own ways. If the Dragons took Chloe, Savage will make sure they pay for it. Calling in the police only gets his daughter killed and we can't let that happen." Just the thought of something happening to sweet Chloe made him want to tear something or someone apart.

"So what, you're just going to go in there, guns blazing and get her out?" Viv questioned.

"No," he said. "That will be a violation of my probation. Besides, she's only seven and that might put her directly in the middle of an already bad situation. I'm going in there to do a little recon and ask if they have her. If they took her, it's for a reason and they'll want their demands met for the exchange to happen." Things like this happened all the time between rival clubs; usually because of one club getting in the way of the other's business. He knew that Savage Hell was a pretty clean club but it was made up of mostly one-percenters and he had a feeling that some of their dealings stepped on the Dragon's toes. Savage would have to intervene and make things right, but he would get his daughter back once all the demands were met.

"She's only seven?" Viv asked.

"Yeah, and the sweetest kid I've ever met—albeit bossy as shit." Kill laughed at the memory of her telling the big, bad MC men in her life exactly what to do.

"How did you meet Savage?" She asked. He knew Viv was trying to decide if the risk he was taking was worth it but he knew it was. He'd walk across fire to help his buddy.

"I met him when I was a kid. He knew my dad and when my family moved here, Savage helped my father find work—you know odd jobs here and there. It was enough to keep my family here and for the most part, we were happy. When my parents went back to Ireland, Savage took me under his wing and even when I had to go away, for my part in stealing that car, he stood by me," Kill said.

"So, it was his club that you were trying to prove yourself to then?" Viv questioned.

"No," he admitted. "Savage wouldn't let me join Savage Hell. He said I was too young and hot-headed and he didn't want any trouble in his club. I think that and my Dad's death were what sent me into a spiral. I wanted to prove to him that he was wrong about me. I knew if I could show him that a club wanted me and that I could be a valuable part of them, he'd want me in Savage Hell. God, I was a fool. Instead, I ended up trying to become part of a club that wanted nothing to do with me. The Dragons were the ones who set me up to get caught. I thought that they wanted me but I was fecking wrong. Hell, they were the ones who helped land me in prison but Savage stood by me the whole time."

"So, you are going to put yourself and your freedom in danger to go back into a club that set you up? What happens if these Dragons decide to do the same to you again, Cillian? What happens to us—to me? I can't stand by and watch you rot in prison; I just found you," Viv sobbed.

Kill wrapped his arms around her, hating that he was hurting her, but there was no other way. "Savage is my family," he whispered. "He's the only family I've got left." Kill wanted to tell her that he felt the same way about her, but now wasn't the time. They were still so new to each other and he worried that making a declaration like that—promising her more than he might be able to give her, wouldn't be fair to Viv.

"You said he lives close by with his husband and wife?" Viv asked.

"Yeah," Kill said. "Bowie is a great guy. He's active military and stationed at Redstone Arsenal. He and Savage met about a year ago and they've been together since. And well, how they hooked up with Dallas is a long story, but they put her between them and it just works for the three of them. Savage and Dallas had a kid together too—Greer. They hooked up before he and Bowie did but he didn't know about his kid. Again—long story."

"What about Chloe's mom?" Viv asked. She pulled free from Kill's arms and had begun fidgeting with the mess on her desk.

"She's dead," Kill said. "Savage is Chloe's uncle. He adopted her when she was just six months old, after his sister, Cherry, and her husband died in a car wreck. Chloe was in the car with her parents, asleep in the back seat but she doesn't remember a thing. She didn't have a scratch on her but her parents both died instantly."

"God, that's awful," she said. "She's lucky to have Savage. I had my grandmother after my mom died and my dad took off," she said. "I guess I was lucky too." Kill couldn't stand the distance she was putting between them. He knew Viv enough to know that she was avoiding him and he hated that.

He pulled her back into his arms, tossing the pile of papers she was clutching against her chest back to her desk. "Talk to me, Viv. Tell me what you're thinking," he demanded.

Her sigh said just about everything for her. "I'm thinking that you need to help your friend and get that little girl back, but I'm not going to lie—you talking to the Dragons worries me."

"I get that, Honey. I can't promise that everything will be okay, but I have to do this." Viv nodded and he gave her a quick kiss. "Wait, was that our first official spat?" Kill asked.

Viv giggled, "I think it was," she said.

"Well, I hear makeup sex is all the rage now," he teased. "You want to give it a go?"

"You mean here? In my office," Viv choked.

Kill eyed her desk and gave her his best evil grin. "I think it looks pretty sturdy," he said. Kill lifted Viv onto her desk and loved the way her breath seemed to catch when he pulled her against his erection, letting her feel every inch of him through both of their jeans. He was perpetually hard around her and was pretty sure he'd never get enough of sweet Vivian.

"What if someone comes in?" Viv questioned.

"Hold my place," he ordered. Kill liked the way Viv didn't seem to take her eyes off him as he rounded her desk to lock her office door. He decided to give her a little show and remove his t-shirt on the way back around to her and Viv's greedy eyes roamed his upper body, taking him all in. Over their past few months together, she had asked a good many questions about his ink. He liked the way she seemed to take an interest in him. It felt so good having a woman like her in his life now.

"You know this is breaking our pact?" he breathed. "The one where we would remain strictly professional at work? You still think this is a bad idea?" he asked.

"Yes," she admitted, letting her hands freely roam his torso. "But, I don't give a fuck anymore," she sassed.

"Good," he said. "Because I've been dying to do this all morning." He pulled her against his body and tugged her shirt up over her head, exposing her bare breasts. "I knew you weren't wearing a bra," he accused. "I'm betting you know how crazy it drives me when you forgo undergarments," he said.

Viv held her thumb and pointer finger up and squinched them together. "Maybe a smidge," she teased.

"You're a minx," he growled, palming her breast. "I think you might need me to teach you a lesson on teasing me," he said. Viv smiled up at him as if letting him know she was on board for any lesson he might want to teach her.

Kill sat back down in her office chair and pulled her half-naked body over his lap. "Straddle me," he ordered. "And for the love of feck, tell me you aren't wearing panties under that mini skirt of yours." Viv did exactly as ordered and straddled his lap, giving him a shy smile and a coy shake of her head.

"For feck's sake," he growled. "You are going to kill me, woman." Kill quickly unzipped his jeans letting his cock spring free and Viv lowered her body over his, allowing him to completely enter her drenched core. Her greedy pussy took him in and Viv rode him as if she couldn't get enough.

"This is all that matters, Viv," he said. "What's happening between the two of us—as long as we have this, I can do anything." He meant it too. When he was released from prison, he thought about doing something stupid to go back. Hell, it was what he knew and Kill knew the statistics. Many felons were repeat offenders because they didn't know how to cope with life on the outside. But Savage set him on the right path and once he met Viv, he wanted to be a better man; not just for her but for himself. She made him that—a better person, even in just the short time they had known each other.

"I know," she stuttered. "I just can't lose you—not now." Viv framed his face with her hands and looked into his eyes and he swore he could see into her soul. All her raw desire and need stared back at him and if he wasn't mistaken, he could see love in her beautiful blue eyes.

"Baby," he crooned, pushing her blond hair back from her face. He pulled her down to kiss her and she moaned into his mouth. He could tell that she was close and he was sure he wouldn't last too much longer. He stood with her in his arms, pulling her from his cock and turned her to face the desk.

"Palms down and ass out, honey," he ordered. Viv was always up for an adventure, especially when it came to what he wanted to do with her body. She seemed to like his alpha tendencies and he had to admit, he was glad. He didn't know how else to be around her.

Kill pushed her down on the desk, facing away from him and thrust back into her body. She moaned and pushed her ass back against his cock, taking everything he was offering and begging for more.

"Shit, baby," he growled.

"I'm going to come, Cillian," she cried out. They weren't quiet and he was sure that everyone in the diner would be able to hear what they were up to in Viv's office, but he didn't give a shit.

"Me too, Honey," he admitted. "Come for me, Viv," he ordered. She cried out his name and Kill could feel her wet core spasm around his cock. He thrust twice more into her body and lost his seed inside her.

"Cillian," she said. "I need—" Viv paused and he worried that he had done something wrong.

"Was I too rough?" he asked. He turned Viv in his arms and looked her over as if inspecting her body. She was still wearing her mini skirt, hiked up around her waist and she looked well sated.

"No," she said, smiling up at him. "I like it rough and you never disappoint. We need to talk though," she said, clearing her throat.

"About?" Kill asked, cocking an eyebrow at her. Viv found her shirt on the floor and pulled it back on, righting her skirt. "If I remember correctly when a woman says it's time to talk, she's either breaking up with the guy or pissed off about something. So, which is it?" Kill zipped up his jeans and tugged his t-shirt back on.

"Neither," Viv whispered. "But, you might be pissed after I tell you what I need to."

"Let's have it," he ordered. "I'm a rip the band-aid off fast kind of guy."

Viv nodded and looked down at the floor, avoiding making eye contact and he hated the way she was trying to hide from him. "Viv," he warned. He put a finger under her chin and gently raised her face until he could look into her eyes. "Don't hide from me," he said.

"Fine," she said around a sigh. "I'm pregnant." It felt as if all the blood rushed to his head making his ears ring.

"Maybe I didn't hear you correctly," he said. "Did you say you're pregnant?" Viv nodded and looked down at her feet again and this time, he let her hide from him. Hell, he wanted to do the same thing, but he felt as though he couldn't move.

"I'm so sorry, Cillian. I have no idea how it happened," she cried.

"I thought you were on the pill." He knew he sounded unreasonably upset but he couldn't help it. He had just gotten out of jail and a baby wasn't something he planned on so soon. He was just starting to get his feet under him and now he was going to be a father?

"I am on the pill—well, I was. When I found out about the baby, I had to stop taking them," she said, swiping at the tears that fell freely down her face.

"How long have you known, Viv?" Kill growled.

"A couple of weeks now," she admitted. "The doctor said that the pill isn't one hundred percent effective. I'm so sorry, Cillian."

"Shit," he shouted. "And, you're just telling me this now?"

"I tried to tell you," she sobbed. "But, every time I did, I chickened out. I'm so sorry. You don't owe me anything and if this isn't what you want—"

"What I want?" Kill shouted. "What I wanted was to get my bearings and acclimate to being out of prison. I wanted to make a life for myself and maybe earn enough money to open a garage, but now that won't happen." He sounded like a first-class ass but he didn't care.

"You never told me about wanting to open your own garage," she said.

"Yeah well, it was just a pipe dream anyway. I took some classes while in prison and I'm a certified mechanic. I thought it could be my fresh start," he said.

"It still can be," she said. "We'll make it work, somehow." She reached for him and he dodged her. Viv let her arms drop to her side, looking completely defeated.

"Okay," she said. "I get it—this isn't what you signed up for. Listen, I'm good. I can take care of myself and this baby—you owe us nothing, Cillian." Viv brushed past him and grabbed her keys and jacket, slamming the office door on her way out.

"Damn it," Kill shouted. He thought about going after her but he wasn't sure that was the best idea. He had royally fucked everything up between them and chasing Viv now wouldn't do him any good.

How could he be stupid enough to let this happen? Kill knew that he should have used a condom but she assured him she was on the pill and taken care of. He trusted her and why wouldn't he? Viv took him in and gave him a job when no one else gave him a second look. She saw the man inside of him and not the felon who had just gotten out of prison. She had given him a chance and when she needed him, he treated her like shit. That stopped now. He needed to find her and make things right before he lost one of the best things to ever happen to him.

# VIVIAN

Viv walked home just as fast as her legs could carry her, a part of her hoping Cillian would catch up to her and the other part praying he didn't. She knew that dropping the bombshell that she was pregnant might end in an ugly argument, but Cillian had all but told her to get lost after she shared her news. She was just as shocked as he was by the positive pregnancy test, but she had a couple of weeks to absorb the fact that she was going to be a mom.

She was so careful, making sure she took her pill every day, but her doctor told her that she was that magical one percent that got pregnant on the pill. Just her fucking luck! She was ready to call it a day, she was so tired. She got home and didn't bother to even take off her jacket, running up to their room and locking herself inside. If he wanted to treat her like shit, he could just sleep in the spare room because there was no way she would let him into their bed tonight—not after he pushed her away like that.

Viv stripped and started the shower, letting the water run hot before stepping into the spray. She cupped her barely noticeable baby bump and sighed. "Looks like it's just you and me, kid," she whispered. When the doctor told her the results from her blood work, she had to have him repeat them. She had gone in for a little cold that had her feeling run down. He decided to run some blood work, never telling her that he was including a pregnancy test.

At first, she thought about aborting the baby and not even telling Cillian. She wasn't quite ready to be a mom and their relationship was still so new, she didn't know how it would even work. Her track record in the relationship department wasn't the best. She already had one failed marriage that ended in divorce. How was she supposed to make this thing work with a man she barely knew and take care of a new baby? But the more she thought about terminating the pregnancy, the more she knew she'd never be able to go through with it. This baby was hers and letting him or her go wasn't an option.

Viv heard the front door slam closed and she knew Cillian had followed her back to her house. She finished her shower and shut off the water, wrapping a towel around her body. Cillian tried the doorknob and when he realized it was locked, he banged on the bedroom door, making her jump.

"Let me in, Viv," he growled. "We need to talk."

Viv laughed at the irony of his statement. Those very words are what started this whole mess today. "I'm good, Cillian," she said. "I think we both just need some time to cool off and think things through."

"Please, Viv," he shouted through the door. "I acted like an ass and I want another chance to make things right. Just open the door."

"I think you were pretty clear back at my diner, Cillian. You have a dream of what your future is going to look like and this baby and I aren't a part of your vision. You deserve some happiness, Cillian. This wasn't supposed to happen but it did and it's not your fault."

Cillian fiddled with the doorknob and she heard it pop when he unlocked it. Viv knew her time for hiding was over. He smirked in at her, looking her body over. Cillian's gaze heated, reminding her that she was still just wearing a towel. She pulled it tighter around her body and he shook his head at her.

"I can't talk to you through the door, honey," he said. Cillian grabbed her robe from the back of the bathroom door and helped her into it. "I also can't talk to you when you're standing in front of me wet and naked. But make no mistake, Viv—we will be talking this out."

"There's nothing more to say," she said.

"That's where you're wrong, Baby. There's everything left to say. I acted like an ass and I'm so sorry. You just caught me off guard and I needed a few minutes to catch up. You've had a couple of weeks to figure this all out but I just heard the news today." He pulled her down to sit next to him on the bed and she had to admit, having him close made her relax a little. Viv wasn't sure why that was. She had never really been around another person who made her feel so at ease. Her ex-husband never made her feel the way Cillian did and that scared the hell out of her. Her ex's cheating nearly destroyed her. What she felt for Cillian was so much more.

"I'm sorry I didn't tell you when I found out," Viv whispered. She shivered and Cillian wrapped his arm around her, tugging her against his body. "I wasn't sure what I wanted to do about the baby and I didn't want to tell you about him or her until I could decide."

"What do you mean, do about it?" he asked.

"I mean that I considered an abortion but when it came right down to it, I knew I'd never be able to go through with it. I want this baby, Cillian. If you don't, that's fine. I can make it on my own. I've gotten pretty good at being alone since my divorce," Viv said.

Cillian stilled beside her and she groaned, wanting to inwardly kick herself for her verbal diarrhea. They hadn't discussed her dating and sex life. Hell, it was a topic Cillian seemed to avoid. Viv knew about his past, for the most part. He admitted that he hadn't been with a woman for the past ten years and she didn't need for him to account for his sex life before going into prison. Viv was happy being left in the dark when it came to Cillian's ex's but from the look on his face, he didn't feel the same way.

"You wanna run that by me again, Viv?" he asked. "You were married?"

"Yes," she grumbled. Viv stood to pace the floor, needing some space from Cillian's warm body. "I was young and stupid. God, I was so fucking naive. I thought he loved me, but our whole marriage was a complete lie. He used me—I was safe and convenient for him. He fucked every other woman in his life, including my best friend and his secretary. Although, I didn't find out about him and Mel, my now ex-bestie, until a few months after our divorce was final. It was poetic really, the way he waited until they were secretly married and just back from their honeymoon, to tell me that they were not only together but had been throughout our whole marriage. She was my Maid of Honor for shit's sake," Viv growled. "That bitch was sleeping with him the whole time we were married and I had no clue. That was my fault though."

"How can your husband being a douche be your fault?" Cillian asked.

"Because I was stupid enough to forgive him after I caught his ass cheating the first time. I came home early from the diner one day to find Jason in bed with the town whore. He convinced me that she meant nothing to him and that he just slipped up. We went to counseling together and I even forgave him, like the fool I was."

"You're not a fool, Vivian. You're a kind, forgiving woman—but not a fool." Cillian stood to look at her and she hid her face in her hands.

"I thought we were good until I walked into his office and found his secretary on her knees, under his desk, giving him a blow job. I left there, packed up all his shit and threw him the fuck out. I was done. I filed for divorce and it was easily granted. I thought I was over all of that but dating proved me wrong. I had major trust issues and even went to therapy again, to work on them. I never really trusted any man that I was with, after Jason," she admitted.

"Oh," Cillian breathed.

"Until you," she whispered. It was the truth. Until she met Cillian, Viv had flitted in and out of relationships, never willing to hear the guy out if she had even an inkling of doubt that he was on the up and up.

"You can trust me, Viv," Cillian said. He framed her body with his hands, hesitant to touch her. He acted almost as if he was waiting for her to push him away or deny him. That wouldn't happen. Viv needed Cillian, whether she wanted to or not, but she wouldn't force him to be a part of her or their baby's lives.

"I know, Cillian," she whispered. "But, me trusting you doesn't mean that you are obligated to be a part of our baby's life. I understand if you don't trust me after I've kept the truth from you. I just needed time to figure everything out," she admitted.

"I get that," he said. "I just wish you would have told me sooner. Two weeks is a long time to know something and not share it. Especially when it could change the other person's life so dramatically."

"I know," she murmured.

"You remember our first night together?" Cillian asked. Viv let her eyes meet his and she smiled.

"Yes," she breathed. "It was the best night of my life," she admitted. It was true too. Being with Cillian felt easy and right. They had only known each other for a few hours before they fell into bed together and it was the one thing in her life she had zero regrets over. Cillian made her happy.

He dipped his head and gently kissed her lips. "Mine too," he admitted. "You said that you wanted a husband and kids," he reminded.

"I remember," she said.

"And, I said that I wanted a few kids too but was always too afraid to let myself hope for something like that while I was in prison," he said. Viv nodded. She remembered the sadness she felt for him when he admitted that to her. She could almost feel his loneliness every time he talked about his time in prison.

"I want that still, Viv. I want a family and kids and God help me, woman, I want all of that with you. I screwed up earlier. I was being a douche and I'm so sorry," Cillian said. "Forgive me?"

Vivian wiped at the hot tears that fell down her cheeks and nodded. "I do," she said.

Cillian made a humming noise in the back of his throat that made her giggle. "Christ woman," he barked. "I can't keep up with all the mood swings. One minute you're pissed at me, the next you're crying and now, you're laughing."

Viv cupped her little belly and looked down her body. "I'm blaming all that on the kid," she said. Cillian gingerly reached his hand out to cover hers and she smiled up at him.

"Give me a chance to be this baby's dad," he asked. "I know that I have nothing to give either of you, but say you'll marry me and we can be a family, Viv." Her guy looked so hopeful; Viv could see in his eyes that he meant every word. He wanted her and their baby and for now, that would be enough for her. She'd worry about Dragons and motorcycle clubs later. For now, Cillian was asking her to be his and there was only one word she could give back to him.

"Yes," she agreed.

# CILLIAN

Kill had taken the day off from the diner to meet with Savage. His Viv had spent the last few mornings sick as a dog, and this morning was no different. At least now he knew what or in this case, who the culprit was—his kid. She was supposed to go with him to Savage's house and meet the family and go over the plan to rescue Chloe, but she was in no condition to meet anyone. Instead, he showed up feeling torn between the promises he made to her and the oath he took to protect his best friend and his club. Savage Hell was his family and not helping his friend went against everything he believed in.

As soon as Savage spotted him through the sea of tattooed bikers, he crossed the bar to pull him in for a bear hug. "Sorry I haven't been around much, man," Kill said.

Savage released him and stood back. "It's good, man. You're doing what you should be Cillian. You're finding your way and I'm so happy for you." Kill noted the sadness in Savage's eyes and it was hard to take, seeing his friend so broken. Kill hadn't told anyone about Viv being pregnant yet but he knew that if anyone tried to hurt his woman or his kid, he'd want to tear them apart.

"What can I do to help?" Kill asked.

"I know the guys came out to talk to you about going into Dragon's territory. I hate to ask you to do any of this man. You're violating your parole," Savage said.

"You let me worry about my fecking parole and tell me what you need from me." Kill cross his arms over his chest, waiting Savage out.

His friend smiled for the first time since he got there. "Thanks, man," Savage breathed. "I knew I could count on you. Honestly, you're the only one who can do this."

Kill looked around the bar at all the able-bodied bikers and back to Savage. "Why's that?" he questioned.

"We've had some trouble with the Dragons, just before you got out. They came after my family and beat the piss out of me. We were hoping things had died down. Dante took off for Mexico, or that's what we had heard and now I think he has my daughter." Savage's voice cracked and Kill knew his friend was on the verge of losing it.

"Dante?" Kill asked.

"Yeah—he's the Dragon's new Prez and has vowed to either kill or patch all Savage Hell's members. He has a personal vendetta against me and the club."

"I don't know him," Kill admitted.

"No, you wouldn't. The guy who was president when you tried to patch into the Dragons has been long gone for years. Dante is the third since he was killed." Kill whistled and shook his head. He had no love loss for the guy. In fact, after what he did to Kill, he fucking hated the guy.

"How'd it happen? Hopefully something gruesome and painful," Kill said, rubbing his hands together.

"Shot to death in his own bar's parking lot," Savage said. Kill felt a little disappointed thinking that his arch-nemesis might have had a quick death.

"Well, let's hope this Dante fellow meets a more painful demise," Kill said. "Tell me how I can help get your daughter back," he said.

"You aren't patched into Savage Hell," Savage said. It was a fact that Kill was painfully aware of. The club had accepted him as a sort of honorary member but beyond that, there was no patch ceremony in prison, just the promise of the club's backing. That was enough for Kill too, until now. Now, he wanted to be a part of something much bigger than his daily existence. He wanted to know that his woman and kid would be watched after and cared for if something happened to him. Savage Hell could be that for him if his damn probation wasn't standing in the fecking way. He couldn't patch into a club for two years now and that sucked.

"Right," he said. "I'm not a patched member."

"Well, the Dragons will know that too," Savage said. "We can use that to our advantage. You can show up at their bar under the guise that you want to prospect and get intel on Chloe's whereabouts."

"That club is all one-percenters, Savage," Kill said.

"No offense man, but you'll fit right in. They've had her for almost two days now." Savage said. Honestly, he wasn't offended. He was worried that if he got caught, they'd throw his ass back in jail and he'd loose the family he always wanted.

"How about I just reach out to my contact in there? Havoc is a good guy and he'd tell me where Chloe is, if he knows," Kill offered. "I can't just walk into that bar. It would be suicide, man. I'd be throwing away everything —Vivian and the—" He stopped short of telling Savage his news. Viv made him promise to keep it just between the two of them until she was further along. She'd have his balls if he just blurted out that he was going to be a father.

"And?" Savage asked. When Kill pressed his lips together, trying to hide his smile, Savage knew what he was covering. "Fuck, man," Savage growled, pulling him in for another bear hug. "You're going to be a father?"

"Yeah," he sighed. "But, Viv made me promise not to tell anyone, so you didn't hear it from me."

Savage held up his hand, "Not a word, man. That's fantastic news, right?"

"It is," Kill agreed. "And also the reason I can't put my freedom in jeopardy. I think we can work out a way for me to meet with Havoc and not raise too much suspicion. The guy runs a gym in town and I can hire him as my trainer. No one would be the wiser and I'm sure I'll be able to get some information from him. As I said, he's a good guy and he'd never want any harm to come to your Chloe."

Savage called over Ryder and Repo, filling them in on their conversation. The three of them agreed that Kill's plan was worth a shot. Kill knew he couldn't stick around the bar for long. Just having his new bike parked out front would land him in a shit ton of hot water. It was time for him to head out and back to Viv.

"I have to go, man. I can't be caught here and I promised Viv I'd be home in time for dinner," Kill said.

Savage looked over Kill's shoulder and swore. "Fuck, man. You need to go out the back," Savage said. "Don't look now but your parole officer is here." Kill knew better than to turn around and give himself away. "Go, Cillian. I'll hold him off for you."

"Thanks, Savage," Kill said. He made his way back through the crowd and chanced a look back to find that Repo, Ryder, and Savage had effectively blocked his parole officer's view of the back of the bar.

"Hey guys," Savage shouted over the crowd and music. "This guy here is looking for Cillian James. Anyone see him around tonight?" Kill smiled to himself knowing that no one would come forward and admit to seeing him, even if they had. It was part of their code and one that could mean being stripped of their patch and put on probation. The guys took loyalty to their club very seriously and even though he wasn't a patched member, Kill knew that included him.

There was a soft murmur in the bar and Kill knew he was good. Savage would keep Hart talking and Kill would be long gone before he got bored and gave up. His probation officer had no clue what he was up against but Kill had a feeling Savage would help him figure it out.

"Sorry man," Savage shouted at the guy. "But, as I said, Cillian isn't here." Kill walked out the back door and found his bike. He popped the clutch and rolled it away down the road, not wanting to draw attention to himself with the hum of the motor. When he decided he was far enough away from the bar, he started her up and started for home. He was going to have to talk the plan over with Viv but he was pretty sure she'd be on board with it. It was a promise he made her when she agreed to be his wife. He would keep her in the loop and she'd never have a reason to distrust him.

---

He found her asleep on their sofa and sat down on the edge of the seat, leaning over her body to kiss her forehead. She had no idea how much he loved her. Hell, they hadn't even given each other the words yet. He knew she loved him too. Kill could see it in her eyes every time she looked at him but he wouldn't force her to say it. Viv had agreed to be his wife and that was enough—for now.

Vivian stretched and smiled up at him. "You're back," she said, her voice groggy from sleep. "What time is it?"

"It's just past six," he said, checking his watch. "Did Jackson Hart show up here tonight?" Kill asked. Viv sat up and looked a little green. "Lay back down, Love," he ordered.

She did as he ordered and smile at him. "I like my new nickname," she said.

"Nickname?" he asked.

"Yeah, you've started calling me, 'Love'." Kill nodded, not wanting to get into all that right now.

"Good," he said, gently kissing her lips. "You're still queasy?" he questioned.

"Yes," she breathed. "I read that Saltine crackers might help with that though."

"I'll run to the store and pick some up, along with dinner," he offered.

"Thanks," Viv said. "And, to answer your question, no. Your parole officer hasn't been here tonight," she said. "Why?"

God, he hated that he was going to have to worry her, but he promised his honesty. "He showed up to Savage Hell, while I was there. I think he's following me, Viv. I can't explain it but it feels like the guy has it out for me."

"Shit," she said, trying to sit up again. Kill pushed her back down and held her there.

"No," he barked. "Stay put. I didn't want to worry you, but I promised to tell you the truth, no matter what."

"I appreciate that, Cillian," she whispered. "Did he see you at the bar?" He hated the worry and fear in her blue eyes, he saw staring back at him.

"Nope," Kill said. He smiled remembering the runaround Savage gave the guy. "Savage and the guys had my back and I got out of there unnoticed."

"Thank fuck," Viv said.

Kill gently palmed her little belly. "You know—when this little one gets here, we're both going to have to watch our swearing." Viv giggled and nodded. "We can't have his first word being, 'fuck'."

"Or, 'feck'," Viv countered.

"Fair enough, Love," he said. "You get some more rest and I'll run to the store. I'll be back in two shakes," he promised. Viv nodded and cuddled down into the sofa. He covered her with the blanket she kept thrown over the back of the couch and she yawned.

"When you get back, you're going to tell me about your meeting," she said. "I know you're avoiding telling me, Cillian, but I'm strong enough to handle this," Viv promised.

"When I get back," he promised. "Just rest now," he said. He stood over her until Viv closed her eyes. She was right, he was avoiding worrying her. He had done enough of that in the last ten minutes. What his woman needed now as sleep and Saltine crackers and that was exactly what she was going to get.

# VIVIAN

A pounding on the front door woke Viv up from her nap on the family room sofa, leaving her feeling a little dazed and confused about how she got there. The last thing she remembered was Cillian kissing her goodbye and leaving to get her some Saltines.

Someone pounded on the door again and Viv sighed and sat up, her stomach roiling in protest. "This better be fucking good," Viv grumbled. She stood and felt a little dizzy, reaching for the wall to steady herself. Her impatient visitor banged on her front door again and she wanted to tell whoever it was to go the fuck away.

"Coming," she shouted. "Hold your fucking horses." Viv hobbled to the front door, her stomach protesting with every step, and pulled it open to find Cillian's parole officer on the other side. He didn't look very happy to see her and she felt about the same way, him having interrupted her nap.

"Hart," she said. "What can I do for you?" Viv held onto the door, trying to right her world but the entire room felt like it was spinning.

"Where's Kill?" he asked. She hated that Hart insisted on using Cillian's nickname. No one called him that, but she had a feeling Hart was doing it to egg her guy on. It was almost as if he was routing for Cillian to fail. What Hart didn't understand was that she couldn't let that happen. Viv and her baby stood to lose too much if Cillian ended up back in prison. She'd do everything in her power to make sure that didn't happen.

"He's at the grocery store," Viv said. She sounded groggy—like she was drunk and her words were slurred. She just wanted to lay back down again, but first, she needed to get rid of Cillian's pesky parole officer.

"You all right, Miss Ward?" Hart asked. She tried to tell him that she was, but before she could get the words out, the room went dark and the last thing Viv remembered seeing was Hart's concern as he pulled her into his arms.

---

"Viv wake up Darlin'," Cillian's voice crooned. She wanted to wake up, really she was trying but she was so tired. She was warm and cozy and the thought of opening her eyes only to experience the waves of nausea and dizziness, had her clamping her eyes shut tighter. Viv felt as if she was floating on a cloud and that was so much nicer than retching out her guts. Opening her eyes would lead to that and Viv wanted to avoid her fate for as long as possible.

"Maybe you should take her to the hospital," another man's voice whispered. "She didn't look so good when I got here. Has she been sick?"

"That's none of your business, Hart," Cillian spat.

"Listen, man, I know we got off on the wrong foot but I had to know if I could trust you," Hart said.

"Trust me for what, exactly? To obey the rules and just try to live a normal life? Well, I have news for you, Hart, that's all Viv and I want. We want to get married and settle down but you keep sticking your nose in our business at every turn. What the hell do I have to do to prove to you that I'm on the up and up? I don't have time for this right now, Hart. I need to make sure that she's all right." Cillian pulled her hand into his own and she could feel him tremble. Viv hated that he was worried about her and Cillian was right—she needed to wake up and call her doctor. They needed to make sure that the baby was okay.

"Cillian," she croaked.

"I'm here, Love," he breathed. Viv didn't make a move to sit up, knowing full well that if she did, she'd be sick all over again.

"Saltines," she whispered. Cillian pulled the box of crackers from one of the bags and opened a sleeve, handing them to her. "Thanks," she said.

"I called the doctor and he said to eat them slowly while lying flat. If you can manage some water or ginger ale, that might help too. I picked up a bottle while I was at the store. That's why I took a little longer than promised. He said that if this doesn't help, he wants me to bring you in so he can check on the baby."

"Baby," Hart questioned. "You're pregnant?"

"Shit," he swore. "Sorry, Love." Cillian turned and stood to face Hart. "Yeah," he admitted. "Viv and I are having a kid. Although, I still don't see how any of this concerns you, Hart."

"Everything you do concerns me, James. Hell, I'm the reason you got out early and I'm also the reason you haven't gone back in yet. I know you've been in contact with your MC," Hart accused.

"I've told you before and I guess I have to say it again," Cillian spat, pointing his finger into Hart's chest. Viv worried that this wasn't going to end well for either of them but she was too weak to do anything but let the whole scene play out. "I don't belong to an MC. I'm not a patched member of any club. I'm close friends with the president of Savage Hell, but you already knew that. Savage was the one who collected me the day I got out. He and my father were close and Savage is like an older brother to me. Seeing him doesn't violate my probation," Cillian said.

"No, but showing up at Savage's bar earlier today does. Most of those bikers are one-percenters, Kill," Hart said.

"What did you mean when you said you're the reason Cillian got out early?" Viv asked. She was nibbling at her crackers and drinking the bottled water that Cillian had given her.

Hart sighed. "We need your help, James," he said.

"What the feck is going on?" Cillian cursed. "Why that hell do you need my help, Hart?" Viv had a feeling that she wasn't going to like Hart's answer.

"We need you to use your connections with the Dragons to get on the inside for us," Hart said. "That's why I've been trying to gauge if you can be trusted or not. I've been following you around for weeks now, and today, when you disappeared into thin air, I assumed you went to Savage Hell. But, I was wrong."

Cillian looked between Hart and Vivian and she worried that he was going to do something stupid. "Cillian, don't," she warned. "How do we know you're on the up and up here, Hart?" Viv asked. She sat up and Cillian hurried over to her side, helping her into a sitting position. She closed her eyes, waiting for the onslaught of nausea, but this time, she felt nothing. "I'm good," she promised him.

"You can't know that I'm being honest with you," Hart admitted. "I'm not a parole officer," he said. "I'm a detective and while I've been assigned to keep an eye on you, James, it's because of your connections. We believe the Dragons are running a trafficking ring and we need to shut it down. You might be the only person who can get in the club, on the ground level and find us the evidence we need to put their president, Dante, away for good."

"Shit," Cillian growled. "Human trafficking?" Hart nodded and Viv felt sick again, but this time for different reasons. If Hart was right and the Dragons were trafficking women, she worried what they would do to little Chloe. She placed her hand protectively on her belly.

"Chloe," she whispered. Cillian pulled her against his body.

"Who's Chloe?" Hart asked.

Cillian sighed, "She's Savage's daughter. He thinks that the Dragons took her two days ago."

"Fuck," Hart swore. "If that's true, we don't have much time. Dante moves shipments across the border every Tuesday. That leaves us just three more days before he could move your friend's daughter. Can you set up a meeting between me and Savage?" Hart asked.

"He won't like it, but yeah," Cillian agreed. "Savage doesn't want the authorities involved. He said that usually causes more trouble than good."

"Well, it's a good thing that I don't want the authorities involved in any of this either. Honestly, I've been undercover while trying to find my way into their organization. I give you my word that the Dragons won't suspect a thing, Kill," Hart said. Viv worried just how much they could trust Jackson Hart. He had been riding Cillian's ass for weeks now and if he was truly trying to figure out if he could trust her guy, he had a strange way of going about it.

"What do you say, Love?" Cillian asked, looking at Viv. She loved that he brought her in on his decisions and always kept her in the loop. Even after she promised that she trusted him, he went the extra mile to prove he was trustworthy.

Viv shrugged, "I trust you Cillian. If you think this is a good idea, then I will follow your lead. Isn't it up to Savage and his family though? They are the ones losing the most if Hart double-crosses us." She chanced looking up to find one very pissed off police detective hovering over them. "You can't blame me for feeling this way, Hart. You haven't exactly been forthcoming with either of us. Hell, up until a few minutes ago, we thought you were a parole officer. It's just a lot to take in."

Hart backed down and nodded. "I get that, Vivian. You are right, I wasn't truthful about who I am, but I give you my word that will change from here on out. Just get me the meeting with Savage and I can prove that I'm on the up and up."

"Fine," Cillian said. "I'll set it up for the morning. First, I have a meeting with an old friend, Havoc. He's with the Dragons and I think he'll have intel on where they're keeping Chloe." Cillian shot Hart a mean smile, "Don't worry yourself about it, Hart. Havoc isn't a felon and he won't be violating my probation. He owns a gym in town and I have a four A.M. class with him. He's agreed to be my trainer and if I can persuade him—my informant."

"Stay in touch," Hart ordered. "Let me know what time Savage wants to meet and where. I'll be there." Hart turned to leave and just before he got to the front door, he called back over his shoulder. "Congrats on the baby," he said and shut the front door behind him.

# CILLIAN

Kill barely slept the night before and his three-thirty wake-up call was a rude reminder of that fact. Viv had been able to keep some broth and crackers down and her doctor said that as long as that keeps happening, she and the baby should be fine. Still, Kill worried that worrying about him and this whole mess with Savage and the Dragons might be putting too much stress on her and the pregnancy. He wanted to make things as easy as possible on her.

"Hey man," Havoc said, meeting him at the front of the gym.

"Thanks for fitting me in so quickly," Cillian said, shaking his old friend's hand. He and Havoc had known each other before he went away. They were both prospects for the Dragons at the same time. They had gone through shit together, both hoping to patch into the MC and when Havoc realized what had happened to Cillian, he felt like shit. During his trial, it came out that the Dragons had not only set him up but were cooperating fully with the local authorities to put him away for a very long time. Havoc was one of the only guys to show up to support him from the Dragons. By that time, he had patched into the club and was a full member, so coming to the courtroom and throwing his support behind Cillian was a major deal. It almost got him kicked out of the Dragons.

"I heard you got out, Cillian," Havoc said. "I'm not sure what the hell to even call you, man. I heard about what went down in there."

Kill knew that Havoc had heard about him killing another inmate. Everyone had, even though it wasn't true. Most people just assumed he did it, even though his friend Capone took the blame for it. There was no use in trying to convince everyone he was innocent. Besides, he didn't give a shit what other people thought or believed to be true about him—never had.

"Doesn't matter to me—Kill or Cillian. Whatever you're comfortable with," he said.

Havoc looked around his gym and back to Kill. "How about we stick to Cillian?" he questioned. "I don't' have a lot of clients at this time of the morning, just some die-hard fitness nuts. Let's not scare them off, just yet," Havoc joked.

Kill smiled and nodded, "Fair enough."

"So, my receptionist said you asked specifically for me and seemed interested in hiring a personal trainer. Tell me more about what you're looking for," Havoc said. That part wasn't a lie. He was hoping to get back to the gym and continue with his daily weight routine but he wanted to add some cardio. A personal trainer would make things so much easier, but he was there for so much more and telling Havoc that might not play out well for him.

"I'm looking to get back into lifting. I haven't had time to find a gym since getting out and your place is close to my woman's house," Cillian said. He needed to gently lead into why he was there.

"Sounds good," Havoc said. "Let's start with some cardio and work our way around the gym to introduce you to the place."

"Great," Kill agreed. He dropped his gear at the front desk and followed Havoc back to the treadmills.

"If you decide to join, we'll get you a locker and you'll have it to keep your things in." Havoc nodded to the treadmill and Kill took that as his cue to jump on. He ran for about twenty minutes and by the time he finished, working his way around to all the machines, going through a full workout, he felt about ready to drop.

"Jesus," he breathed, wiping the sweat from his face.

"I didn't say I'd go easy on you, old man," Havoc teased.

"You do know we're about the same age, right Havoc?" Kill asked.

"Well then, shit." Havoc slapped him on the shoulder. "You have a fucking lot of work to do to catch up, man. How about you hit the shower and meet me in my office. I'd like to talk to you about maybe running a few weight classes for me. We have a lot of guys from some of the area MC's who come in here to bulk up. You have that part of the routine nailed. With some cardio, we can have you in fighting form in no time. How do you feel about teaching some boxing? I know you were really into that, back in the day." Kill smiled remembering the time that he and Havoc sparred in the ring.

"Yeah. As I recall, I kicked your ass," Kill teased.

Havoc chuckled, "Yeah, yeah. You were in better shape back then. I'd like a rematch," he teased, puffing out his chest and flexing. Kill laughed and grabbed his bag.

"You're on," he agreed. "Just not today. You've kicked my ass enough for one day. Let me shower up and then we can talk," Kill said. Teaching boxing and weight classes wasn't the path he had seen for himself, but honestly, he wouldn't hate it. He could work at the diner and help Viv out there during the day and then teach a few classes in the early morning and evening. The extra money would help him to get one step closer to his dream of opening a shop and working on cars. Hell, if he could work on cars and continue to teach boxing, it would be the best of both worlds.

Kill quickly showered and joined Havoc in his office. "Have a seat," Havoc offered, shutting the door behind Kill. "Listen, the job is yours if you want it. I could use the help around here. But, I need to talk to you about something else, too."

Havoc slunk down into his chair and Kill knew he wasn't going to like what his old friend had to say next.

"I'm out of the Dragons," he almost whispered. Kill wasn't sure he had heard Havoc correctly.

"Come again," Kill said.

"I'm out," Havoc said, clearing his throat. "Of the Dragons. They stripped me of my patches when I refused to follow orders. I was put on probation, but I told them that they could shove that up their asses."

Kill whistled, "That was ballsey," he said.

"Ballsey—fuck, it was damn stupid. I'm constantly looking over my shoulder now. This week has been one fucking mess and I'm not sure who I can even trust anymore."

"Why tell me all of this?" Kill asked. "Hell, you don't know that you can trust me, now do you?"

Havoc nodded and fiddled with some papers on his desk. "No," he said. "But, I'm hoping that I can. You see, I think you're here for the same reason why I was ousted from the Dragons. They took Savage's kid," Havoc admitted.

"Feckers," Kill said, standing from his seat. "They have Chloe?"

"Yeah," Havoc breathed. "I was part of the crew they sent to take her. They went by her school, during recess and well, they took her. I never showed to help with that part and when Dante found out that I bailed, he stripped me of my patches. I'm fine with not being a part of the Dragons anymore but I'm not all right with what they plan to do with that little girl."

"What's Dante planning?" Kill asked. He was worried that he already knew, but he had to hear it from the horse's mouth.

"They are going to ship her to Mexico. Dante's running a trafficking ring and he specializes in virgins. That poor kid will be sold off to the highest bidder and I just can't stand by and let that happen. You still close with Savage?" Havoc asked.

"Yeah," Cillian said. "He's partially why I'm here." Kill held up his hands, "Don't get me wrong, I'm all in on this gym thing and I'd love to teach for you. But, I thought you might be able to give me a little information about the Dragons—you know two birds and one stone?"

Havoc shrugged, "Sure."

"How long do we have before they move her?" Kill asked.

"I'm not sure," Havoc admitted. "I was kicked out a couple of days ago now and I've been out of the loop. Honestly, I've been laying low. We both know that the Dragons don't just let you leave. It's only a matter of time until they either suck me back into the club or I disappear." Havoc was right, Kill did know how the Dragons operated all too well. He had been on the losing end of their shenanigans and that was a place he didn't plan on ending up again. This time, he had an ace up his sleeve—Jackson Hart. He wouldn't fail to use his safety net if need be. There was no way he'd let the Dragons win again. He had too much to lose and Viv and their baby were worth fighting for.

"We'll just need to make sure that doesn't happen, Havoc," Kill said. "I've got your back."

Havoc barked out his laugh, "Considering the fact that I never had your back, I appreciate that, Cillian."

"The past is just that—the past. I won't hold you responsible for the shitty decisions I made and you can stop beating yourself up for not having my back. You were the only guy who spoke up for me and the only one who showed up to support me at my trial. I'll not forget that Havoc," Kill promised.

Havoc held out his hand and Kill took it. "When can you start teaching classes?" he asked.

"How about next week?" Kill asked. "I just have a few odds and ends to work out and then I can jump right in. Thanks for the opportunity, man."

"Not a problem, Cillian. I appreciate you taking this on. Will I see you tomorrow for training?" Havoc asked.

"Yeah," Kill agreed. "But, for the love of Christ, can we meet any later?"

Havoc chuckled, "Sure. How about six? That time work better for you?"

Kill groaned. "Yes," he said. "It's still early but will give me time to shower and get to work. See you at six," Kill said. He turned to leave Havoc's office, grabbing his gym bag on the way out.

"Yep—six, sharp," Havoc called after him. Kill waved over his shoulder, not bothering to look back. He knew he'd find his old friend watching him, wearing his shit-eating grin that was always infectious. Kill made Havoc a promise to have his back and that was one he planned on keeping. He had just enough time to swing by Savage's house before he had to be home to help Viv at the diner. Kill wasn't looking forward to having to convince Savage to hear Jackson Hart out, but it might be the only way to get Chloe back knowing that there was now a ticking clock hanging over their heads. Time was of the essence and they would all need to work together before it was too late.

---

"You fucking mean to tell me that you went to the cops, Cillian? Why the hell would you do that when I specifically told you not to? You know how these things run. We take care of club business and leave the cops out of it," Savage growled. Cillian watched as the big guy paced the floor in front of the bar. Bowie and Savage met him there when he called, leaving Dallas and the kids at home. Cillian told them he had news and they didn't want the kids in on their conversation. They were just babies but Greer had asked about her sister a few times and Dallas had told her she was at a friend's house. It broke Cillian's heart that they were all having to go through this but Savage needed to remember the end game—getting Chloe back from the Dragons in one piece. Nothing else mattered.

"Just hear me out, Savage," Cillian asked.

"No—just fucking no," Savage growled.

"Maybe we should just all calm down and hear Cillian out, Babe," Bowie offered. "It can't hurt. If you still want to kill him when he's done, I'll help." Bowie shot him a wolfish grin and Kill nodded his thanks. He could tell that Savage's husband was just trying to soothe him and from the way Savage exhaled and sunk into a chair, it seemed to be working.

"Fine," Savage grumbled. "Start talking."

"I went to see Havoc," Kill said.

"You should have led with that, from the beginning," Savage said. "What did he say? Does he know if they have my daughter or where they are keeping her?"

"Yes," Kill breathed. "He said they have her and last he saw her; she was safe and being held by the Dragons."

"Last time he saw her?" Savage asked.

"Yeah, he didn't have much to go on since he's out of the Dragons. He refused to be a part of Chloe's kidnapping and they stripped his patches and he walked," Kill said.

"Fuck," Savage shouted. "Why didn't he warn me?"

Kill knew exactly why Havoc wouldn't rat on his old club. "They'd murder him if he had. Hell, they would have probably killed Chloe by now if Havoc ran to you, just to make an example of you both. You know how they operate better than anyone, Savage. The Dragons don't play by the rules. Havoc still has to watch his ass. They won't let him just walk away from their club, but he's out—for now."

"So, we're back to knowing nothing?" Bowie asked.

"Well, there's more and this is the part that you both aren't going to like very much," Kill admitted.

"I haven't liked one fucking word you've said so far, Cillian," Savage griped. "Just spill it."

"Havoc confirmed that Dante is running a trafficking ring and he specialized in virgins. He's planning on moving Chloe to Mexico and selling her off." Kill watched Savage like he was a bomb about to go off.

"What the fuck," Bowie shouted. "We have to stop them from doing that, Savage. If they move her, we'll never get Chloe back."

"Don't you think I know all that, Bowie?" Savage almost whispered. He sounded defeated and even broken. Cillian hated that anyone had the power to bring his friend to his knees.

"So, we don't let that happen," Cillian said. "We take Hart up on his offer and I go into the Dragons. I can work on finding Chloe once I'm on the inside and get her out. We don't have time to sit around and think about this though, Savage."

"She's just a little girl." Savage's voice broke and it nearly gutted Cillian.

"I know man. This is the only way. Let me tell Hart that I'm in. It's like you said yesterday, I'm one of the only ones who can do this. The Dragons will think that I'm desperate to be a part of a club and they'll believe I want to prospect to join them. Once I get into the club, I can find Chloe and get her out of there," Cillian said.

"Just like that?" Savage asked. "You honestly believe it'll be that easy?"

"Yep," Kill lied. He was sure that it would be a shit show but he wasn't about to tell Savage that. His friend had seemed to lose all hope and there was no way he'd let Savage give in to his despair.

"I can't lose her," Savage choked. "You have no idea how much this hurts."

"I get it, man, I'm not a father. But, I will be soon. I know that if anything happened to Viv or the baby, I'd be lost. At least let me try," Kill said.

Bowie nodded at Savage and the two seemed to share a silent connection. "Fine," Savage agreed. "Set up the meeting for this afternoon. You'll go into the Dragons tonight and ask to probate. If they are going to move her, I want you in there to stop it. I won't lose my daughter," Savage growled and stood. He walked out the back of the bar, not bothering to look back.

"Sorry," Bowie said. He stood and slid his chair under the table. "That's great news about Viv and the baby, Cillian. He's just not ready to hear anything goodyour right now. We need to get Chloe back—for all our sakes."

# VIVIAN

Cillian came running through the front door with about ten minutes to spare before they needed to head out to the diner. She had felt like shit and had spent most of the morning bowing to the porcelain god. Luckily, the trick her doctor told her finally started to work and she was able to keep the crackers and ginger ale down.

"Sorry," he said. "I met with Havoc and then had my ass reamed out by Savage."

"You can't blame the guy. You would be just as upset if it was your kid," Viv said.

"I'd kill every fecking one of the Dragons if they took our kid," he said, cupping her belly. "How are you feeling today?"

"Same," she said. "But, better now. I foolishly got out of bed when I should have eaten my Saltines before my feet hit the floor. I think that might help. I just need to remember to put them on my nightstand before I go to sleep from now on."

"I think I can handle that chore," he said. "You already do too much, Viv. You need to let me pick up some of the slack both here and at the diner, Love," he offered. Viv smiled at the way he called her 'Love'. Cillian had been doing that a lot lately and she had to admit, each time made her feel like a giddy schoolgirl.

"So, did Savage agree to meet with Hart?" she asked. Changing the subject was her safest bet. She and Cillian hadn't professed their undying love towards each other, even though she just wanted to blurt it out so many times. They had other pressing matters to worry about and then, she'd find a way to tell Cillian she was in love with him. He had asked her to marry him and she had agreed but a part of Viv worried that was just for the baby's sake. At least on his part. She was in love with him, baby or no, and marrying Cillian just felt right.

"Yep," he said. "I called Hart on my way home and we'll meet at Savage Hell at noon."

"What about your parole?" Viv asked.

"Hart said that I would be considered working and cooperating with an undercover operation and all of my parole rules would be overlooked," Cillian said.

"Wow," Viv breathed. "Is this safe?" Cillian rummaged around the refrigerator, looking for something to eat and she could tell he was avoiding having to look at her.

He made a humming noise in the back of his throat that told Viv all she needed to know—it wasn't safe. "Shit, Cillian," she shouted. "If you are walking into a dangerous situation, don't you think I have a right to know about it? I am the mother of your child."

He closed the fridge and crossed the small kitchen to pull her into his arms. "You're right, Love," he said. "And, don't forget you're going to be my wife." Viv smiled up at him and nodded. That was something she couldn't forget because she wanted to be Cillian James' wife more than anything.

"Yes," she murmured. "So, if you go off and do something stupid and get yourself killed, I won't get that chance." Viv buried her face in his jacket and snuggled into his arms. "Please don't do anything stupid, Cillian," she whispered.

"I promise," he said, not missing a beat. "I have you and this baby now. I wouldn't chance either of you for the world. Just give me a little trust here, Viv. You'll see." She knew she could trust him. He was honestly the first man she had trusted in a damn long time but his promises weren't ones he could keep. Dealing with the Dragons was going to be dangerous whether she liked it or not. Cillian could make her every pretty promise he could come up with but that wouldn't change the fact that he wasn't in control of what the Dragons would do to him if they figured out what he was up to.

"I'm going in tonight," he said.

"Tonight?" she sobbed. Cillian sighed and nodded.
"Please Viv," he begged. "Don't make this any harder than it has to be. I give you my word that I'll come back to you."

Viv pulled free from his arms and gathered her stuff for work. "Don't make me promises you can't keep, Cillian."

"Where are you going?" Cillian questioned. Viv opened her front door, not bothering to look back at him She knew if she did, she'd stay. Seeing the hurt in Cillian's eyes that she heard in his question would be her undoing and she'd cave. Viv knew that her only option for protecting her baby and her heart would be to walk out that door and not look back, no matter how hard that was to do.

---

Viv watched the clock cursing under her breath each time she realized that only a minute or two had passed since the last time she looked at it. "You okay, Boss?" Tommy asked. New Kid was working out surprisingly well. Viv had stopped calling him that to his face since he had been with the diner as long as Cillian had and that felt like a lifetime. A lot had happened in just mere months, but she felt as though she had known Cillian her whole life.

"Yeah," she lied and plastered on her smile. She'd keep the fact that she was worried that she'd never see the man she had fallen in love with—the man who held her whole life in his hands—again after tonight. She didn't believe for one-second that Cillian walking into the Dragon's bar and declaring he wanted to be a prospect was a good idea. Viv was certain it was a fucking awful idea but how could she stop him from going? She couldn't. An innocent little girl's life was at stake and she'd feel awful if she stood in the way of Chloe being safely rescued.

"Is Cillian coming in today?" Tommy asked.

"No," she said. "He has some errands to run today," she lied again. Viv looked up when the bell sounded over the front door, to find a big guy with dark hair and tattoos that ran up his arms, walking in. He reminded her of Cillian and her heart sank.

"You can sit anywhere," she called to the guy and he nodded, taking a seat in the corner booth. Tommy grabbed a menu and a silverware bundle and Viv took, them both from him. "I've got this one," she said. "You take the couple over there." Tommy nodded and grabbed two more menus.

"Sure, Boss," he said.

Viv looked the hot tattooed guy over, noting the way he watched her. "Today's special is a BLT club with fries," she said. "Can I get you something to drink?" What she wanted to ask the guy was why he had wandered into her little diner. She was beginning to get the feeling that it wasn't a coincidence at all. Viv looked back at the clock that hung over the back counter and realized that it was about time for Cillian's meeting with Savage and Hart.

"Coke," he said, drawing her attention back to him. "Please."

"Sure thing. I'll be back in just a minute to take your order," Viv said.

"No need," he said. "I'll take the special." Viv nodded and went back to the kitchen to put in the order. She was so used to having Cillian back there that when she found Cole behind the grill, she felt a little disappointed. In such a short time, Cillian James had infiltrated every aspect of her daily existence and she worried that she'd never be able to find her way forward without him. Viv pulled her cell from her pocket, thinking about calling or texting him, but that would be a mistake. Cillian had decided to put himself in harm's way and she wasn't going to just let him off the hook for that. She needed to stand her ground no matter how stubborn that made her sound.

Viv grabbed the Coke and walked back to the corner booth. Biker Guy looked her over and smiled. "You all right?" he asked.

"Yep," she lied. "Just worried about a friend." God, Cillian was so much more than her friend but explaining that to a stranger wasn't her scene.

He chuckled and sipped his Coke. "If Kill heard you call him your friend, he'd be pissed." The guy stood from the booth and Viv had to crane her neck to look up at him, he was so tall. "I'm Repo," the guy said, holding out his hand. Viv shook his offered hand, not sure if she should be afraid of the big guy or call him a friend.

"You know Cillian?" she questioned.

"Yep," Repo said. "I'm in Savage Hell."

"So, you're a friend of Cillian's?" Viv asked.

"Yes," he breathed. "He sent me over to keep an eye on you and help out in any way that I can."

"Well, Repo is it? I don't need your help or your protection. I'm fine on my own. What I needed was for the man I love—the father of my baby—to listen to me, but that didn't happen. Cillian decided what was going to happen for himself and didn't consider my feelings in this matter at all."

"Listen," Repo said. "I know this has to suck for you but Kill can handle himself. He knows what he's doing and he won't go off and do anything stupid."

"You mean like get himself killed and leave me and his baby to fend for ourselves?" Viv spat.

"That won't happen," Repo said. "Savage Hell will always care for you and Kill's kid. You're family now and we take care of our own. That's why this is so important to him—you know, helping Savage get his kid back. We're all brothers and when someone comes for one of us, they have to deal with us all."

Viv sunk into the booth across from Repo. "I get that, I do. I know I sound like a heartless bitch, but I just found Cillian. I can't lose him now. I appreciate that you are trying to keep an eye on me, but that's not necessary. I'm sure that I'm safe. I'd much rather you have Cillian's back than mine right now."

"See, that's where you're wrong, Honey," Repo said. He sat back down and gave her an easy smile. "Once Kill goes into the Dragons tonight, you'll be a target. He knows that and asked me to keep an eye on you. They will hunt down everyone who means something to Kill.

I'm assuming I'm looking at the most important person in his life. Well, two people," he corrected. "How about you let me do what I've been ordered to do by my club's Prez and you just forget I'm here?"

It was going to be damn near impossible for her to simply forget the giant tattooed man sitting in the corner, but what choice did she have. Viv had a feeling that no matter how much she protested; he wasn't going anywhere.

"Fine," she said, standing again. "Lunch rush is about to start and I don't have time to argue. Do what you want—stay, go, I don't give a fuck." Viv turned to walk away while Repo's chuckle filled the corner of the diner. "Tommy," she shouted loud enough for Repo to hear. "Table six is all yours."

# CILLIAN

"You sure about this?" Savage asked. Kill wasn't. But, telling his friend that walking straight back into the pits of hell, to rescue his little girl, scared the shit out of him, wasn't something he could do. They had been over the plan a half dozen times now and every time he looked at Savage, Cillian saw that damn hope in his eyes. It was enough for him to push aside his fears and agree to this suicide mission because that was exactly what walking into the Dragon's bar was. Cillian knew that if the tables were turned and it was his kid they had; Savage would do the same for him.

"Yeah," Cillian lied. "It's going to be a piece of cake, right? I'll just go in, pretend I want to prospect, find Chloe and get the fuck out of there." Cillian looked between Savage, Bowie, and Hart, knowing from the expressions on their faces that they weren't buying a word he was saying.

"Shit, Cillian, Savage grumbled.

"It's fine, really," Cillian said. He had his poker face in place, not wanting to let his friend know just how much he hated their plan. All he could think about was the way Viv walked out on him earlier that morning. How she hadn't even given him the chance to tell her that he was in love with her and that he wanted his chance to do that. Now, he might never have that opportunity again and that scared the shit out of him. It also gave him the strength to push through and make his way back to her. He had to tell her that she now held his heart and his future. Viv and their baby were driving him to pull through whatever lay ahead and make it out the other side.

"I'm going in with you," Hart said. "You'll need someone on the inside who has your back and the Dragons don't know me."

"Now wait a minute, Hart," Cillian griped. "You can't just go and change the plan now that we've worked it through."

"I can and I just did. You can't go in there without back-up, man." Cillian knew Hart was right but the thought of his former probation officer, now turned police detective, having his back seemed laughable. "Don't look at me like that. I told you why I was riding your ass these past few months."

"Yeah, yeah," Cillian said. "You had to make sure you could trust me. What if I'm not so sure I can trust you, Hart?"

"How about me? You trust me?" Havoc asked. He stood in the back of the bar as if he was eavesdropping on their whole conversation.

"Fecking hell," Cillian shouted. "You can't just knock like a regular fecking person?" Havoc chuckled and pulled up a chair to the table they sat around. "Sure, help yourself," Cillian grumbled. "Everyone this is Havoc."

"Good to meet you all. I've heard good things from Cillian," Havoc said.

"Wish we could say the same," Savage said. "What are you doing in my bar, Havoc?" Savage mean mugged the guy and Cillian knew that having a former Dragon in Savage Hell wasn't his friend's idea of a good time. Still, Cillian trusted Havoc with his life and knew that if he had to go into Dragon's territory with anyone, he'd want it to be him.

"I'm here to help," Havoc admitted.

"Help how?" Bowie asked. "Weren't you just kicked out of the Dragons?"

"Yep," Havoc said. "For not kidnapping your kid."

Savage stood and growled, slapping his palms down onto the small wooden table. Cillian worried that there meeting was going to end badly. Bowie put his hand on Savage's arm, "Just hear him out, Babe," Bowie said.

"Fine," Savage barked. "But, make it fast so I can toss your ass out of here and we can get on with saving my daughter."

Havoc had the nerved to smile and Savage looked about ready to punch his smirk right off his face. "I know I didn't stop it from happening but I couldn't go through with Dante's plan to take your kid. You have to understand that telling him no put a price on my head. I couldn't just run to you and tell you about his plan—he was having me watched. If I would have shown up at Savage Hell, he would have killed Chloe to make an example out of us both. I decided it was best to lay low. That was until Cillian showed up at my gym this morning. I can't let what they have planned for your daughter, happen. So, I'm here to help."

"While I can appreciate the danger you're in just by showing your face here, I'm still confused as to how you think you can help," Hart said.

"Dante has issued me an ultimatum. I either go back to the Dragons and accept my punishment on probation or I'll be dealt with." Havoc shrugged as if that threat meant nothing to him.

"When?" Cillian asked. "When did you know about this?"

"A day," Havoc admitted.

"And you didn't think to share that bit of information with me?" Cillian questioned.

"I wasn't sure what I was going to do when I saw you this morning. I've given it some thought and decided that you walking into that place by yourself is going to end up getting you killed. I can't let that happen, man. I let you walk into a set up ten years ago and look how that ended for you. You spent ten years in prison and I could have prevented it if I had just stepped up and stopped being a shitty friend. I knew that they were setting you up and I know that you going into the Dragons now will get you killed. Let me do the right thing here, Cillian."

Cillian had suspected Havoc knew about the setup but hearing him confirm it gave him an unexpected sense of relief. "I told you before that stealing that car was on me. I made that choice and you beating yourself up about it, all these years later, isn't worth it. I did my time and now, I'm ready to make different choices—better choices." Cillian shot Hart a look and nodded. "I say he's in."

"How would this work?" Hart asked.

"I'll go in with a peace offering—two prospects. Dante will eat that shit up. He'll love the fact that I potentially poached Cillian from Savage Heat and you'll just be considered a bonus. We need to come up with a back story for you—maybe make you new to the area or something. If Dante even gets a whiff of you being a cop, he'll slit all three of our throats, no questions asked."

"Let's get to work then, we have a lot to do before tonight's meeting," Cillian said. "I have my woman covered but I'd appreciate your promise that if anything happened to me, you'll take care of her, Savage."

Bowie stood and held out his hand to Kill. "You have my word," he swore.

"And, mine," Savage said. He stood and pulled Cillian from his seat, bear-hugging him until Kill was sure he'd have to tap out.

"I can't breathe, Savage," he protested. Savage chuckled and released him.

"You're family, Cillian. That extends to Viv and the baby. We'll always take care of them both," Savage promised. Kill felt a little choked up at the mention of being considered a part of Savage's family. He had to admit, it felt pretty damn good to be a part of anything again. Family was hard to come by and Cillian would do just about anything for his—even go on a suicide mission.

---

Kill, Hart and Havoc parked their bikes in the back of the bar's lot and cut their engines. Cillian eyed the bar suspiciously as if it would remember him the way he remembered his days as a Dragon's prospect. He hated the kid who wanted to be a part of something so badly that he threw his entire fecking life away. Cillian knew that sooner or later he'd have to forgive himself for being that stupid kid. But, for now, his hatred was what was fueling him to go through with this whole crazy plan.

"You good man?" Havoc questioned.

"Yeah, just stick to the plan and don't feck this up," Cillian warned, looking directly at Hart.

"Don't look at me, man. I've got this down pat. It's just another Thursday night for me. You two need to calm the fuck down and stop looking at me like you don't trust me. If we're going to be believable, we have to at least pretend to like each other," Hart said. He wasn't wrong. Cillian didn't trust him and if Dante or any of the Dragons caught on to that, they'd all be dead.

"Fine," Cillian said, slapping Hart on the shoulder for good measure. "Let's do this, Old Friend."

Havoc chuckled and shook his head. "You two pussies are going to get me shanked, I just know it. Let's get this shit storm over with. I've got some groveling to do and if I'm lucky, Dante will just have his guys knock me around a little. While that's happening, you two have a look around, to see if you can find Chloe. Ready?" Cillian hated knowing that Havoc was going to have to endure a little pain for their plan to work but there was no way around it. He knew how things worked—you went up against the club, you ended up dead or wishing you were.

"Ready," Cillian lied. He let Havoc take lead and he and Hart flanked his sides. They made their way through the side door and into the main room of the bar. There was a full house tonight, probably of guys who were there to watch some retribution. Word usually got around fast and if it was made known that Havoc was coming in to grovel, guys would show up to watch.

"Well, look who decided to take me up on my generosity. You brought friends, too." Dante shouted over the music and hum of conversations. Everyone in the bar stopped talking and turned to see who their Prez was talking about. The sea of bikers parted, letting the three of them pass and Havoc seemed to take that as their invitation to approach Dante.

He sat up by the bar in a booth that Cillian would guess was made especially for him. It seemed to sit higher than the others and allowed him to look over everyone in the crowd, much like a king would sit on his throne over his subjects. They stood in front of Dante's makeshift stage and Kill felt like he was holding his fucking breath for what was about to come next.

"You here to join us or to accept your fate?" Dante asked. The crowd hummed with excitement at the prospect of there being a punishment doled out tonight for their viewing pleasure.

"Join," Havoc shouted. Some of the guys booed and hissed and Havoc laughed like he was enjoying their shouts of disapproval.

"You know you can't just quit the Dragons and not pay some price, right Havoc?" Dante yelled.

Havoc nodded and pointed to Kill and Hart. "That's why I brought you a peace offering, Prez," he lied. "Two prospects." Kill and Hart stepped up, flanking Havoc's sides again. Cillian wasn't sure if Dante looked pleased or pissed at the idea of him waltzing back into his club with two guys at his side. He could take them being with Havoc as peace offerings or as a threat. However he took it would be up to him and Kill knew that Dante's word would be law. He also knew that the leader of the Dragon's was ruthless, after hearing how he went after Savage's family months back.

"I heard you were out Kill," Dante said, looking him over. He wasn't surprised that the Dragon's Prez knew who he was. It was Dante's business to keep tabs on everyone linked past and present to the club. "I just had you pegged on joining Savage's gang of pussies," Dante taunted.

Cillian smiled, trying for cool, even though he felt anything but. "Nope," he said. He knew not to speak until spoken to, as a prospect. He had been through this process before with the Dragons. The only problem was the last time, it didn't end so well for him. "I've found that Savage Hell isn't who I am anymore, since doing my time. Let's just say that I've gotten a little harder after being in prison. I think the Dragons are more my speed now."

Dante looked him over as if sizing him up and nodded. He turned to give Hart the same attention and Cillian's damn heart felt as if it was going to beat right out of his chest. "And who do we have here?" Dante questioned.

"This is Fuzz," Havoc said.

Dante laughed, "What the hell kind of name is that?" he asked.

"The kind that you get when you used to be a cop," Hart said.

"Shit," Cillian swore under his breath. Dante nodded to his enforcer who stood just off to the side and he stepped forward and punched Hart in the gut.

"You'll find that you learn the rules quickly around here," Dante growled. "Rule one—you don't speak unless I ask you to, prospect. Got it?" Hart was still doubled over, holding his gut and when he didn't immediately respond to Dante, he had his enforcer land another punishing blow—this time to poor Hart's jaw. He groaned and straightened, trying to look Dante in the eyes.

"Answer me, prospect," Dante ordered. "What's rule one?"

"No talking unless you ask it," Hart offered. He wiped at the blood that dribbled down his chin and Cillian felt bad for the guy.

"So, you were a cop?" Dante asked. "What makes you want to join the dragons, Fuzz?"

Hart's smile was mean, "To kill some fucking cops," he said. Dante looked him over, trying to decide if he believed the guy or not and then threw back his head, laughing.

"I think I might like you, Fuzz. That is if you can learn the fucking rules." Hart nodded at Dante, keeping his mouth shut. Yeah, it didn't take much to learn the rules when they were beaten into you enough. Kill had learned that lesson in prison.

Dante nodded to his enforcers again and two moved to stand behind Havoc. Kill could feel the tension rolling off his friend's big body and he knew what was going to happen next.

"I'll accept your peace offering, Havoc. But, you're still a little short. How about you agree to be our pre-show before the main attraction starts tonight?" Havoc stared Dante down, his smile was mean.

"What'd you have in mind?" he asked.

"You fight my two enforcers, in the cage. You win, you get to stay. You lose and I kill the three of you." Havoc looked at Kill and nodded back up at Dante.

"Deal," he agreed.

Dante clapped his hands together and a cheer went up through the bar. "Perfect," Dante shouted. "That gives us just enough time to prep for our little auction." Cillian looked around the bar, trying to figure out what Dante meant about having an auction. He didn't see anything laying around for sale and he had a sick feeling that whatever, or in this case, whoever Dante was going to sell off wasn't in the room yet.

"Take them downstairs and throw them into the cage. Get the girls ready. I've promised our guys a preview before we sell them off. Remember guys," Dante shouted back to his club. "Highest bidder gets to play with their prize but you can't take their pussy. The girls have to be virgins when we ship them over the border. Mouths and asses are fair game. Have some fun with them—give them a little experience for our customers." Cillian felt sick thinking that one of the girls might just be little Chloe. She was just a babe and the thought of any of those assholes laying one finger on her made him want to tear them apart.

Dante's enforcers shoved them down a flight of stairs into what smelled like a damp, musty basement. Some cages lined the walls and Cillian realized that the musty smell was probably urine. Cillian knew that smell all too well. If he had to bet, those cages were where they held the women and girls they were transporting over the border. They were patted down; their cell phones were taken and the three of them were thrown into a larger cage in the middle of the room. Kill panicked when he heard the clink of the metal doors and the sound of the lock turning.

"Sit tight, guys," the bigger one taunted. The second guy laughed and Cillian watched as they walked back up the stairs back to the bar.

"Shit," Cillian growled. "They took our fecking phones. What do we do now?" he asked,

"My phone is bugged," Hart said. "It's sending our location to my precinct as we speak. They have people in place and once they hear what just went down, they'll send them in. We just have to hold on until then," he whispered.

"How long do you think that will be? You saw how big those guys are. I don't know if I'll be able to handle them both. Dante said if I fail—we all die," Havoc said.

"Yeah, that was hard to miss, man," Cillian whispered. "And, if your guys move in before we can find Chloe then this was all for nothing, Hart."

"Shit," Havoc swore. "So no pressure, but I have to take down two behemoths and do it fast so we can find Chloe?"

"Yeah," Cillian agreed. "You up for that?"

Havoc shook his head and smiled. "You were always an optimist, Cillian," Havoc said. "Whatever happens, we need to find Chloe because letting any one of those assholes touch her isn't going to happen," Cillian said.

"Agreed." Hart nodded to the group of bikers who were filing down the steps and into the basement. They were rowdy and shouting out bets. Money was being collected and Cillian knew his fate was going to be decided in the next few minutes and all he could think about was Viv. He just hoped like hell he'd get the chance to tell her how much he loved her.

Dante walked down the stairs and held up his hands as if demanding everyone's silence. His club quickly quieted and he turned to face Cillian, Havoc, and Hart. "It looks like we have a change in plans," Dante shouted. "Our merchandise has arrived and is ready to be purchased. Since we have so many esteemed guests here with us tonight, I don't want to keep everyone waiting. So, we will have our little match after our auction."

Cillian panicked. If they were caged up for the auction, how would he get to Chloe and get her out of there? "Shit," Cillian breathed. He watched as three young girls were brought down the stairs wearing blindfolds. He knew Chloe as soon as he saw her and the two girls with her didn't look much older than Savage's daughter.

"Bring them up here," Dante ordered. "Gentlemen, we have three young virgins tonight. Remember—I need for them to be verified virgins after they spend the evening in your care. Bidding starts at five thousand dollars and You can use them as you see fit, as long as you bring them back virgins." Chloe sobbed and Dante nodded at the enforcer who was holding her by the arm. The asshole pulled a ball gag from his pocket and put it in Chloe's mouth. Her cries rang through the basement and Cillian wanted to fucking kill the asshole who was hurting her.

"Bid," Hart whispered.

"What?" Cillian asked.

"Bid. If you can purchase the girl, Dante might let you out of the cage. That will at least give you a fighting chance to get her out of here," Hart whispered. "It's worth a shot."

"I don't have money to bid," Cillian said.

"Yeah, you do. Just before we came here today, I had a hundred thousand transferred to your account. I thought we might need to buy our way into the club, so I took the initiative and put the money in your account."

"What about you guys?" Cillian questioned. "And, the other two girls?"

"You get Chloe out and call in back up," Havoc said. The crowd grew louder by the minute and Cillian knew the bidding was about to begin. He had nothing to lose by bidding and hell, maybe the guys were right and that might be their only way to get Chloe out and call in help.

"Here, we have Savage's little girl. Making her yours will be retribution for everything that bastard has put us through." The guys' cheers were defending and Dante held up his hands again to quiet his men.

"The bidding starts at five thousand," Dante said. Cillian watched as hands started raising around the cage and before he knew it, the bid was up to fifty thousand.

"Shit," Cillian growled. "That's half of what you said you deposited."

"Just wait a little longer. Come in at the end and bid it all," Havoc whispered.

Cillian waited and watched as bidding slowed and when they got up to eighty thousand, Dante was about to announce Chloe sold to an older guy who stood in the back of the room.

"If there aren't any more bids," Dante shouted.

"One hundred thousand," Cillian shouted from inside the cage. Dante slowly turned to face the three of them and his amused smirk was deceiving. Cillian could see the threat behind his eyes. He worried that pissing Dante off was the wrong call but in most club's it would go against their code of honor if Dante didn't honor Cillian's bid. His money was as good as anyone else's in the room. The only question would be if Dante would accept it given the fact that he wasn't a guest but more a prisoner at the moment.

"Come again," Dante spat.

"One hundred thousand," Cillian repeated.

"What makes you think you're in any position to bid on my merchandise?" Dante asked.

Cillian shrugged, "I figured my money is as good as anyone's," he said. "That and I'd like a little retribution." Dante looked over as if trying to decide if he wanted to believe him.

"How do I know I can trust you?" Dante asked.

"You don't," Cillian admitted.

"I'll make you a deal, Irish," Dante said. "You take Havoc's place and fight my two guys—you win, and I'll accept your bid."

Cillian knew he wasn't going to get a better offer than the one Dante was offering but taking on Dante's two enforcers and walking out of that fucking cage was going to be damn near impossible.

"And, if I lose?" Cillian asked.

"Then the original rules apply and I kill the three of you and we auction Savage's kid off to the next highest bidder." Cillian looked over to where little Chloe was coward in fear, sobbing quietly to herself. He saw no other way around it. Cillian was going to have to take Dante's offer.

"You in or out?" Dante asked.

"In," Cillian agreed.

"Well, let's do this then," Dante said. He nodded to the two big guys who had thrown them into the cage earlier and they opened the door to climb in. Pulling it shut behind them.

"He gets no help. Either of you interferes and the fight will be over and you forfeit your lives. Understood?" Dante asked. Hart and Havoc nodded and looked at Cillian.

"I've got this guys," he said. Cillian just hoped he was right because now he had not only the guys depending on him but Chloe too and he couldn't let any of them down.

"Shirts off," Dante ordered. This wasn't Cillian's first fight. Hell, he spent most of his time in prison in brawls and that gave him a leg up. Kill had taken down guys bigger than the two standing in front of him. He just never had so much riding on a fight before. Kill watched as the two guys stripped out of their shirts and tossed them into the corner of the cage. He looked them both over, searching for any old wounds that would be a weakness for either man. He noticed what looked like a fresh knife wound in the one guy's side and knew if he landed a few strategic punches, he might be able to bring the big guy down.

The roar of the crowd was deafening in the dungeon-like basement and Cillian knew that chancing a look over to little Chloe was a bad idea. He needed to focus but hearing her cries and sobs made his heartbreak.

"You got this man," Havoc promised.

"And, if I don't?" Cillian countered.

"Then it was a good run," Havoc said.

"Well, lucky for us, I have too much to look forward to. I have no choice but to win," Cillian said. "My woman will have my balls if I lose."

The crowd around them grew louder and Cillian ducked when the guy to his left came out swinging for him. "I guess there are no rules, then?" he shouted at his massive opponent.

"Prison rules," the enforcer shouted back.

"Well then, it's fecking great that I just got out," Cillian said. The guy didn't flinch at the mention of him doing time. Instead, he held up his hands, wiggling his fingers at Kill to "bring it". He knew enough from his boxing days that charging in wouldn't end well with two opponents. If he did, they could sandwich him between their bodies and quickly end the fight. Instead, he knew that dividing and conquering the two would work best. He decided to take care of the big guy first since he seemed eager to get this fight going. Kill punched him in the side, landing his first blow where he had noticed the guy's old knife wound. He could hear a crack as his fist made contact with the enforcer's flesh. The big guy doubled over, holding his side and Kill took that as his cue to finish him off. He grabbed a handful of the guy's hair and kneed him in the face, once making contact with the guy's nose and a second time, nailing him in the jaw, knocking him out cold. His opponent dropped to the concrete floor with a thud and Cillian turned to find the second guy who had been circling him, waiting for his chance to strike.

Kill wasted no time with formalities, he charged the smaller enforcer and started landing blows. He ducked the guys attempt to punch him in the jaw, instead taking the blow to the side of his head. Kill's ear rang and he shook his head, trying to get himself together. This guy was fighting dirty but Kill knew how to fight dirtier. He punched the guy in the stomach and when he doubled over in pain, Kill made contact with the asshole's groin, kneeing him in the crotch as hard as possible. The guy cried out in agony and Kill knew he had him. He punched him over and over in the face, wincing with every blow that ended with a crack. If he was correct, he had broken the guy's nose and his jaw. Kill's knuckles were on fire but he couldn't stop now, he had to finish this or he'd never see his woman again. He made a promise to both Viv and Savage and he planned on keeping them both.

The second guy dropped to his knees, still refusing to yield and Kill had no choice. He snaked his arm around the guy's neck, choking him until he stopped struggling against Kill's body. Kill didn't stop until the guy's arms dropped to his side and his whole body went limp. He wondered if the guy had passed out or if he had killed him. Either way, he couldn't show any weakness, he dropped the guy to the hard concrete floor and said a little prayer that he hadn't just killed a man in cold blood. Kill turned to face Dante, noting the shock he saw in his eyes. If he wasn't mistaken, it was mixed with a little fear and that was just where Kill wanted the guy.

Kill held his arms wide and smiled through the chain-link cage at Dante. "We done here, or do I need to prove my loyalty further?" Kill taunted. He felt as though his whole body was on fire. The two enforcers had landed a few good hits to his face and Kill could feel his right eye swelling shut. All things considered; he was walking away from the fight in pretty good shape.

Dante looked torn as to what to do about the three of them. He looked past Kill to Hart and Havoc and then back to Kill and nodded. "Let them out," he shouted.

"What about my bid—do I get to claim my prize?" Kill challenged. Dante sighed and reluctantly nodded his agreement.

"Fine," he said. "But you don't have her back here by sunrise and I'll find the three of you and finish what my enforcers couldn't"

"You're just going to let us walk out of here?" Havoc asked. He and Hart flanked Kill's sides and stared down Dante.

The Dragon's Prez shrugged and nodded, "Sure. I'll just be sending my guys to keep an eye on what you each hold precious," Dante spat. "I've had a little research done on each of you since you arrived at my bar. Let's just call it insurance that you'll all make the right choices." He pointed at Havoc, "You have a thriving business—a gym you love. You," he said, pointing to Hart, "Fuzz, was it? Well, you are a bit of a mystery to me, but I dug a little deeper and found that you have a little cabin on the outskirts of town and a German Shepherd you have some hottie watching." Hart growled and took a step towards Dante. Kill stopped him, placing an arm across Hart's chest.

"Not worth it, man," Kill whispered.

Dante chuckled, "Yeah, I'm betting the sexy blond watching your dog is more than just a dog sitter to you, Fuzz," he spat Hart's supposed name. "And you," Dante said, pointing to Kill. "You've been quite busy since you got out, haven't you? You have done well, finding a pretty little woman, Kill."

He took a step towards Dante and Havoc threw his arm up, crossing Kill's chest, giving him back his same words. "Not worth it, man," Havoc said.

"We understand the consequences," Havoc spat. "We fuck you over and you fuck up our lives and destroy everything and everyone we love. That sound about right?"

"Sure," Dante said. "Plus, I'll make you wish you were dead and then I'll kill you—all of you."

"Duly noted," Havoc said.

"Great, head upstairs to pay and we'll get your merchandise ready," Dante offered. The crowd started to disperse and Dante's shrill whistle rang through the basement. "We have two more girls to auction off, guys. Don't disappear," he shouted. They brought the two other girls up to the cage and pushed them through the door. Kill wanted to tell them that he'd make sure that they were saved but he wouldn't make a promise he might not be able to keep. They were both blindfolded and gagged, like Chloe and it made him sick to think of any man in that place touching either of them. They weren't much older then Chloe—maybe teenagers and he could smell their fear.

"Bidding will start as soon as we get business settled, sit tight," Dante shouted. He followed Kill and the others up to the bar and Kill felt panicked when he realized he couldn't see Chloe.

"Deep breaths, Kill," Havoc said. "Let this play out." Kill knew his friend was right but he just wished this shit would be over.

"No sweat," Kill lied. They were escorted back to Dante's office and Kill pulled his debit card from his wallet, saying a little prayer that the hundred thousand that Hart said was put into his account was there. Otherwise, he had a feeling that they'd all be facing the same threats Dante had already spelled out for them, just moments earlier.

A few minutes passed and one of Dante's guys came back into the small office and handed Cillian back his card. "We're good here," the guy said to Dante.

"Bring in the girl," Dante said. The guy nodded into the hallway and within seconds, another one of the bikers shoved her into the already crowded office, blindfold and gag still in place. When the guy made a move to take off her blindfold Kill panicked. Chloe would know him. She'd be able to find security in recognizing him. But, if he had them leave her blindfolded, he'd have his safety. He couldn't risk Chloe telling Dante how Kill and her father were close enough to be considered brothers. He couldn't risk their lives that way.

"Leave it," Kill ordered. "The less she sees and whines, the better." The guy looked at Dante as if he needed his permission to take a piss or breathe, for that matter. Dante nodded and Kill took Chloe's arm into his hand. He wanted to be gentle, but he also knew that doing so would give up his façade. He needed to play it cool until he could get her out of Dragon's territory.

"Sunset," Dante said. "Don't forget."

"No problem. Now, if you'll excuse me, my meter's running," Kill said.

Dante's smile was mean. "Remember the rest of the fucking rules," Dante spat, "and we'll be just fine."

# VIVIAN

Viv peeked out the window to find Repo sitting in his pick-up truck across the street, watching her house. He was a fucking dog with a bone and Viv worried that Cillian wasn't going to be home any time soon. That wasn't her only worry—hell, she was consumed by every thought that ran through her head of what could go wrong. She hoped that the call she put into Savage would give her some new news but his husband, Bowie, answered his cell and told her that they had no word. He promised to call her just as soon as he had any information for her but that had been hours ago.

"Where are you Cillian?" she sobbed, cupping her little bump. "Your Daddy is starting to worry me, Baby Bean." There was a soft knock at the front door, startling Viv. "Fuck," she swore.

She pulled the front door open to find Repo standing on her porch. "Can I come in?" he asked.

"Is he all right?" she asked. God, she needed for Cillian to be all right. Viv hated the way her voice wavered. She didn't sound as strong as she wanted to, but she wouldn't hide her worry.

"Kills fine," Repo said. Viv walked into the family room and sunk onto the sofa.

"Thank fuck," she said. "I've been so worried. Is Chloe okay?"

"Chloe's fine. Let me finish Viv," Repo said. "He's alive and he got Chloe out of the Dragon's bar but you need to come with me."

"What? Why?" she asked.

"You're in danger. I'll tell you about it on our way to Savage Hell, but I need for you to grab your things so we can get out of here." Repo stood over her as if waiting for her to make a move to follow his orders. A part of her wanted to protest but the thought of putting herself or her baby in danger wasn't a chance she was willing to take.

"How long will I be gone?" she asked.

"As long as it takes to keep you safe, Viv," Repo whispered. "Kill said to pack some of his things too and close the diner for a few days."

Viv nodded at Repo, "I'll be ready in ten minutes," she promised.

"I'll wait here," he agreed.

Repo pulled up to a house that sat about a half-mile down the road from Savage Hell and Viv unbuckled her seatbelt, anxious to get in to see Cillian. "Viv," Repo said. "Before you go storming in there, Kill was involved in a little fight while he was in with the Dragons."

"Oh God," Viv sobbed, raising a trembling hand to her lips. "You said he was alright."

"He is, but he's a little beat up. Savage's kids are here and little Chloe has been through hell and back. I just didn't want you to freak out," Repo whispered.

Viv nodded, "Promise," she said. All she cared about was getting to Cillian. The rest would work itself out. A big bald man with a salt and pepper beard came out to stand on the front porch and smiled at her. "That Savage?" she asked.

"Yep," Repo said. "Come on. I'll introduce you to everyone and you can check on your guy." Viv got out of Repo's truck and followed him to the porch.

"You must be Vivian," Savage said, holding out his hand.

"Nice to meet you, Savage," she said, letting him take her hand into his. Savage pulled her into his big body and gave her a bear hug that nearly choked the life out of her.

"You mind putting my woman down?" Cillian grumbled. Savage chuckled and released her into Cillian's arms. "Feck I missed you, Baby," he said.

Viv stood back from him and looked him over. "You look like shit, Cillian," she whispered. Viv reached her hand up to gently cup his bruised chin. "Does it hurt?"

"Not much," he lied.

"You're a horrible liar," she teased.

Savage laughed, "She's got you there, Cillian. How about you two say your hellos and then come to find us inside. We have a lot to work out in the next few hours. Sun will be up soon and we'll have to move." Viv watched as Savage disappeared into his house and wrapped her arms around Cillian's waist.

"Are we really in danger?" she asked.

"Yes," Cillian breathed. "I'm so sorry, Baby. I didn't mean to get you caught up in all this. We can't stay here until things are sorted with Dante and the Dragons."

"What happened?" she asked.

"I'll explain everything inside, promise," Cillian said. "But Dante got away when the police invaded his bar. They got the two other little girls though, thank God," Cillian said.

"There were more?" Viv asked. The thought of any young girls having to go through what Chloe did, made her sick. Knowing that they had more than just Chloe was awful.

"I didn't think I'd ever see you again, Love," Cillian admitted. Hearing her call her his special nickname made her heart beat a little faster.

"Cillian," she whispered.

"No, let me finish, Viv," he said. Cillian framed her face with his big hands, pushing her hair back from her face. "I thought that I wasn't going to get out of there. They had me in a cage with Hart and Havoc and I had to fight for our freedom. The whole time I was getting the shit pounded out of me all I could think about was you and our babe," he said, putting his hand over her belly. Viv covered it with her own and they stood like that for what felt like forever, sharing the same space, breathing the same air.

"I love you, Viv," Cillian whispered. "I know you promised to marry me and God, I hope you want to do that because you've fallen for me too, but I get it if this is too much, too soon."

Viv went up on her tiptoes to brush her lips against his own. "I love you too, Cillian." She wouldn't give him anything but the truth.

"Really?" he questioned. Viv giggled and nodded.

"Really," she confirmed. "I have for a while now. I've just been too chicken to say it out loud. I want to marry you because I love you. I just worried you didn't feel the same way. You're the type of man who does the right thing and I guess a part of me worried you were marrying me because of the baby."

"No," Cillian breathed. "You're my family now, Viv. You both are my whole life." Cillian pulled her back against his body and kissed his way into her mouth. "You two love birds about done?" A guy walked up to the porch and brushed straight past them, giving Viv a wink and a smile. He had pulled up behind Repo's truck in his pick-up and she didn't even hear him.

"Havoc," Cillian said. "This is my Viv."

"Good to meet you, Viv," Havoc said on his way into the house. "We're burning daylight, man," Havoc said. "You coming in?"

"Cillian, we can talk about all of this later," Viv offered. Whatever the guys had to plan sounded as if it had an expiration time stamp on it and if she wasn't missing anything, that time was sun-up. Cillian nodded and wrapped a protective arm around her.

"Come on, I'll introduce you to the rest and then we can figure out what the hell we're doing next. You trust me, Viv?" he asked.

"With my life," she agreed, smiling up at him.

---

Cillian introduced her to everyone as "his Viv" and she nearly had to stop herself from swooning. She loved meeting Savage's family and kids. She had heard so much about them. The only person she wasn't able to meet was Chloe since the doctor had given her a small sedative to help her rest. Viv saw the sadness in Savage, Bowie, and Dallas and felt horrible for them. She already felt an unexplained protectiveness for her unborn child. Savage's daughter had been through hell and Viv didn't know what she would do if someone came after her child. She saw how Cillian had gone in to save Chloe and she took some comfort in knowing he'd do the same for their baby if push came to shove. Honestly, the only thing getting her through all of this was knowing that Cillian had her and would do everything in his power to keep her and their unborn baby safe.

"You look worn out, Viv," Cillian said. "How about you rest and I'll let you know when we're ready to move out." She trusted Cillian to make the hard decisions for her but Viv wanted to be a part of this discussion.

"No," she said. "I'd like to be a part of this." Cillian wrapped an arm around her waist.

"You need to rest for the babe," Cillian whispered.

Viv smiled up at him, "I promise to rest later." Cillian nodded, not pushing her further. She was thankful that he let it go with the others pretending not to listen in to their conversation. Viv could feel all eyes on them.

"Listen up," Savage said. Viv was pretty sure the big guy was used to people doing exactly what he ordered. "We have about four hours until the sun comes up and we need to figure out our next move." Savage nodded to Hart who took over their little make-shift meeting.

"Before we went in, I activated the tracker on my cell and my guys heard everything we were saying. When they took my phone, my team got ready to move in. They showed up just after we were clear, going in and making arrests. They got most of the guys who were there and both girls they were auctioning off with your daughter." Hart looked at Savage. "They were only eleven and thirteen."

"Fuck," Savage growled.

"The good news is, they've been reunited with their parents. The bad news is there are more girls out there and Dante and about six of his guys got out," Hart said.

"Shit," Havoc said. "So, Dante's probably figured out what happened by now and he'll be on the warpath. Hell, he told us exactly what he'd be taking from each of us if we double-crossed him. My gym," Havoc whispered.

"I have security measures in place for my sister—that's who Dante found at my place, taking care of my dog. He won't be able to find her; I've made sure of that," Hart said.

"What did Dante say he'd threaten to take of yours Cillian?" Viv asked. She was afraid she already knew the answer to her question though.

"You and the baby," Cillian whispered. "That's why I had Repo bring you here. I can't let you out of my sight, Honey. Dante's coming after all of us and we need a damn good plan to bring that asshole down."

"He won't stop there," Savage said. "He considers my daughter his property and he'll want her back. I think we need to come up with solutions and take a vote," Savage said.

"Well, we can always take off," Bowie offered. "It worked the first time we had to deal with Dante. It could work again. This time, we won't be able to head to Texas since he knows about the house there."

"We can barricade ourselves in here and protect what's ours," Savage said.

"No," Dallas protested. "The kids can't go through that. Chloe has already been through enough. I say we run."

"I'm with Dallas," Cillian said. "We aren't safe here. We'll be sitting ducks."

"But, where will we go?" Viv asked. "Won't we be just as vulnerable out there, with no place to go?"

"She's right," Savage said. "We need a safe, secure place to land. One that Dante has no idea exists. Suggestions?"

"I can fly us anywhere," Ryder piped up from his spot in the corner. "Just say the word."

"The problem is where?" Cillian asked.

Repo stood next to Viv and she could hear his sigh. "I don't go around sharing this, but I have a cabin in Gatlinburg, Tennessee. It can accommodate all of us."

"I didn't know you were from Tennessee," Savage said.

"No one does. In my line of work, I don't share my home address with anyone. I have a place here in town but try to get to the cabin as much as possible. It's yours if you need it, Savage," Repo offered.

"Thanks, man," Savage said. "I think that's going to be our best option if we chose to run. We stay here, we're sitting ducks—I get that. But if we leave, we can be picked off just as easily. Let's put this to a vote, just like club business."

"What about non-club members, Viv asked. Do we get a vote?" She knew that Cillian was considered a Savage Hell honorary member but he wouldn't be able to vote in their meetings.

"This isn't church," Savage said. "Everyone gets a vote tonight. We each have something to lose in this. So, those in favor of staying put and holding our ground?"

Viv looked around their small circle as Savage and Hart put their hand up. "Well, it looks like we're packing up and heading to Repo's cabin then if it's just the two of us."

"I'll have the plane gassed and ready. Remember, I can only take eighteen passengers," Ryder said.

"And, I'll call my housekeeper to open up my cabin and stock it," Repo said.

"Can you trust her?" Cillian asked.

"Him and yes," Repo said. He's ex-Navy and honestly, I'd trust him with my life. Doc's like a brother to me. He watches the cabin while I'm here or chasing down a runner."

"A runner?" Cillian asked.

"Yeah, I chase down people who fail to show up for arraignment—you know, bail jumpers," Repo said.

"I'm familiar with the term," Cillian said.

"Well, it keeps me away for weeks or even months at a time. I don't get home to Gatlinburg as often as I'd like," Repo admitted. Viv noted the sadness in his voice and wondered if he left his home in Tennessee running from something or even someone.

"Fine, get everything in place. We leave in thirty minutes," Savage ordered.

"Can I help you pack for the kids?" Viv asked Dallas.

"Absolutely," Dallas said. "With three kids, I need all the help I can get." Viv smiled up at Cillian and he nodded.

"You go ahead. You'll need the practice of packing for our little one, soon enough," Cillian said.

# CILLIAN

They got to Repo's cabin just after daybreak and he could see just how tired his woman was every time she put on a brave face and smiled up at him. "You look about ready to drop, Love," Cillian said.

"I feel it," she admitted. "Would you mind if I laid down to have a nap?" She asked around a yawn.

"Of course," he said. "How about we rest together? I could use some shut-eye." It was the truth. He had been up for almost forty-eight hours now and he felt like the walking dead.

Repo's cabin was incredible. Savage had called in a few of the guys, from Savage Hell, to travel with them. They were acting as makeshift guards and he was grateful that Savage had thought to bring extra protection. It would allow him the luxury of a few hours' sleep and gave him peace of mind knowing his woman would be safe if he closed his eyes. Even with the full planeload of eighteen people, Repo had rooms for everyone and some to spare. His and Viv's room was at the end of the left-wing and was partially secluded from the main house. He loved that they could have their privacy and Savage's protection at the same time. The threat of Dante's Dragons coming after them was a very real one. His vendetta against Savage was personal and now Hart, Havoc, and he were caught up in that feud.

"That sounds perfect," Viv said. Cillian pulled her into his arms, carrying her around to the side of the bed. He gently laid her on the fluffy comforter and she scooted over, as an invitation. Cillian climbed in next to her and pulled Viv against his body, loving the way she snuggled into his hold.

"This is perfect," he whispered against her neck. He kissed the soft skin behind her ear and she snored softly, causing him to chuckle.

"That's right, Viv. You sleep for now," he said. Cillian closed his eyes and let his exhaustion consume him. He just needed some sleep and he'd feel better about this whole mess. Yeah—he just needed a few hours.

---

Kill woke with Viv's body wrapped around his own and if he wasn't mistaken, she had her hand down his trousers. "What's happening here, Honey?" he asked. Viv gave him her shy smile and if he had to guess, his little vixen had woken up refreshed and ready to play.

"We slept for almost seven hours, Cillian. I'm hungry and horny. I figured we could take care of the latter first. Then, maybe I can convince you to help me find the kitchen and we can grab some food." Viv waited him out, her hand resting on his already stiff cock.

"Shit," he swore. "Well, you do know how to wake a man up, Love," he teased. Viv seemed to take that as her cue to pump his erection in her hands, letting her fingers caress the top of his head. He moaned and thrust harder against her palms as if needing more.

"You like that?" she questioned.

"I fecking love it," he admitted. Kill did too. Every time Viv touched him felt like another piece of him was clicking into place. He knew it sounded cheesy but she did complete him. Vivian Ward was making him who he was and Kill had to admit, he liked the person he was with her. He just hoped he'd live up to his own expectations of being a good father. He'd never be able to stand it if he let Viv or their kid down.

"Cillian," she whispered. "Love me."

"You never have to ask me for that, Baby." Cillian brushed back her long blond hair from her eyes and pulled her body against his, kissing her soft lips. He broke their kiss and she mewled her protest, causing him to chuckle. "I love you, Viv." She smiled down at him, her body still pressed up against his own, her hand holding his cock in her firm grasp.

"I don't think I'll ever get tired of hearing you tell me that, Cillian," she whispered. "Say it again."

"I love you, Viv," he whispered. Cillian peppered her neck with butterfly kisses and Viv shivered against him.

"I love you, Cillian. I never thought I'd meet someone like you," she admitted.

"How so?" he asked. He hated that everything in him believed that Viv deserved better than him. He was an ex-con and Viv was so sweet. She deserved so much more than he was going to ever be able to give her. The one thing he couldn't do was give her up because walking away from Viv and their kid wasn't a possibility for him anymore. He needed her just as much as he wanted her.

"When I was with my ex," she began and Kill moaned. The last thing he wanted to do was talk about her ex-husband with her tangled up in his bed. He wanted to strip her bare and sink balls deep into her pussy, but that could wait a few minutes.

"Just hear me out," she protested.

"Fine—you have two minutes until I get you naked." Cillian liked the way her eyes flashed with need at the mention of getting her naked. She'd be on board for whatever he had planned. His Viv usually did.

"Deal," she agreed and batted her eyelashes at him. Kill chuckled and shook his head. "When I was with my ex, I thought that he was what I deserved. Like I wasn't good enough for anyone else. I was convinced that all men cheat and hell, maybe I even pushed him to do it—you know because I thought it would inevitably happen." Kill opened his mouth like he was going to protest and Viv covered it with her hand. "Please," she said. Kill nodded and she hesitantly pulled her hand free from his lips.

"Go on," he prompted when she made no move to continue.

"I finally got fed up and kicked his ass out. Hell, maybe I thought I was happy on my own, I don't know. I was doing all right without a man in my life. At least that's what I told myself. But, meeting you proved me wrong. I think I was waiting my whole life for you," she whispered.

"Oh Viv," Kill breathed. "I feel the same way." Cillian cupped his hand over her bump and smiled at her. "I never thought that having someone like you would ever be a possibility for me. When I was in prison, I didn't think past the next day. My entire existence was staying alive, day by day, minute by minute. That all changed the day I walked into your diner. You and our baby changed me, Viv. You both made me a better person. I want to be a better man for you both. Thank you for giving me a chance." Cillian didn't give her time to comment. He rolled her under his body and sealed his mouth over hers, stealing her words along with her breathy sighs and soft moans. Viv was the perfect woman for him and if he had his way, he was going to show her just how perfectly they fit together.

He pulled her t-shirt up over her head, leaving her in just her panties. She slid his gym shorts down his body and he rubbed his unruly cock against her wet panties.

"Fuck, honey," he said. "You are already so wet for me, Viv."

"Only for you, Cillian," she promised. She shamelessly thrust her hot core against him and he couldn't take anymore. He slid her panties to the side and sunk into her body. Viv moaned so loudly; Cillian was sure the others would be able to hear her. He kissed her like he couldn't get enough, only allowing her to come up for air when she was gasping and panting with need.

"You feel so good, Viv," he said. He was so close, he rolled her on top of his body, knowing that position usually got his woman off. "Ride me, Honey," he ordered. Viv smiled down at him, throwing her head back and riding his cock as he commanded. She was close and Kill knew that he wouldn't last much longer. He reached down between where their bodies were joined and ran the pad of his thumb over her clit. Viv hissed out her breath and when she came, he felt as though she was milking his cock. Viv cried out his name and he couldn't help himself, he followed her over, whispering sweet praises to his girl.

Viv cuddled into his body and they laid there like that for what felt like an eternity. "Problem one solved," she giggled.

"Problem?" Cillian questioned. His body felt like jello and his sex brain fog still hadn't lifted.

"Yep," she confirmed. "Remember—I woke up horny and hungry. You took care of the horny part but now, I'm starving."

Kill laughed, "Well, we can't have that now, can we? How about you put on some clothes and come with me to the kitchen? I can make us something to eat and then we can watch a movie or something later. Sound good?" he asked.

"Sounds perfect. I'm thinkir appearance soon, Savage will s us," Viv teased.

"You're probably right, Hone body and swatted her ass. "G we'll go make our appearance. out of bed and pulled on her ' Her hair was tousled and she l and completely sated and Kil gotten so damn lucky.

ass, cupping and squeezing her fleshy globes, making her squeal.

"Cillian," she giggled. "Stop, someone will see us." Viv looked around the spacious family room to find both Ryder and Repo sitting in the corner of the room, smiling at the two of them. "Shit," she whispered. "You want to play then take me to our room."

"Well, that sounds like a challenge," he said. "Marry me, Love," he whispered against her neck. Cillian was kissing his way up to her mouth and when he pressed his erection against her belly she gasped, giving him access to her mouth. He kissed her like his two friends weren't sitting in the corner watching them.

"Cillian," she warned, trying to push his big body from hers. "I already told you I'd marry you."

"Sure," he said, shrugging. "I mean now. Marry me now, Viv."

Viv barked out her laugh and Cillian looked hurt. "You can't be serious," she challenged. "We're in hiding from a group of bad guys who call themselves the Dragons. And now you want me to what—run down to the courthouse and marry you? We can't even leave the house, Cillian." He looked so disappointed she wished she could take back her words, but she knew that there would be no way to do that.

"Have you changed your mind about marrying me then?" Cillian asked. How could he doubt her? She'd never change her mind about spending the rest of her life with him.

"Never," Viv breathed. "I'd never change my mind about you, Cillian," she promised. She framed his face with her hands, not caring that they had an audience and kissed his lips. "I love you and that will never change."

"Okay," Cillian sighed. "Then marry me. As soon as this mess is done with and we can get home safely, go down to the courthouse with me and let's get hitched." Viv hesitated, not wanting to hope that they'd ever be free of this mess. She wanted to agree but that would mean taking a leap of faith she wasn't sure she had in her. "If you want a big wedding," he said, "I'm sure we can put it off for a bit until I can figure that out. I'll just have to save up a little first," Cillian offered.

Who would she have a big wedding for? She had no relatives and the courthouse honestly sounded perfect to her. "No," she said. "I like the idea of going down to the courthouse. Besides your club, neither of us has any family. It will be perfect," she promised.

Savage walked into the kitchen and stopped to look between the two of them. "Can't you two take that to your room?" he grumbled. Viv giggled at just how put out he was acting. Savage was constantly touching Dallas and Bowie. She caught the three of them making out on the pool table just the night before.

"You're one to talk," She teased. "As I recall you had no problem getting the eight ball in the corner pocket last night."

"Fuck," Savage swore. "Yeah, well—we thought everyone was asleep and you try being intimate with three kids in your room."

"Chloe's still sleeping in your room?" Cillian asked. Ever since her abduction, she hadn't left Dallas' side. Viv worried that running away from their problems wouldn't ease the little girl's fears. She needed counseling and they wouldn't be able to find that for her while hiding away from the Dragons.

"Yeah," Savage whispered. "She refuses to leave Dallas and I honestly can't blame the kid. She's been through hell and back."

"She has, man," Cillian agreed. "Just give her some time. Once we can go back home, I'm sure you guys will be able to find a family counselor who will be able to help Chloe work through all this."

"I know. I just wish we could do something now to help her," Savage said. He looked between the two of them again and rolled his eyes. "Shit, I'm sorry, Cillian. I went and fucked up your make-out session with my problems. What were you two talking about anyway? Or do I want to even know?" Savage asked.

"Well, we were just talking about our wedding. We're going to go down to the courthouse once we get the all-clear to head home," Cillian said.

"Hey, that's great guys," Savage said.

"Thanks," Cillian said. "You want to be my best man?"

Savage seemed a little choked up, nodding his answer. He patted Cillian on the back and pulled him in for a quick hug. "I'd love to be your best man, Cillian," Savage said. "Thank you. How about you let Savage Hell throw you a little party after. You know, nothing too fancy, but we'd like to celebrate you two getting hitched."

"We'd love that, Savage," Viv agreed. "Thank you." Cillian smiled at her and pulled her against his body. Thanks, man," Cillian said. "That would be lovely."

---

Another week had passed and Viv was bulging out of her regular clothing. She needed to pick up some new pants, preferably with stretchy waistbands, as soon as possible. Convincing any of the guys that it was a necessity and not a luxury wasn't going to be easy.

Enlisting Dallas' help might have been her finest idea in a damn long time and when she searched the room that Dallas, Savage, and Bowie were sharing, she found Dallas napping on their big bed with Greer and the baby. It was probably the cutest thing Viv had ever seen and she rubbed her little belly. She often wondered if she would be a good mother, especially now that she was around Dallas, who was a fantastic mom, and her kids. Watching her friend with her children had her doubting her abilities and Viv hated that.

She had always been the type of person to face any challenge head-on, never backing down from one. When her grandmother died, she picked up the pieces and did what was expected of her, taking over the diner and making it her own. She loved that place too, but it wasn't her original plan. Hell, nothing in her life was as she had planned it to be. It was all better—the diner, moving into her grandmother's little house and now, meeting Cillian and having a baby together. It was all so much more than she could have ever imagined. But, that didn't stop her panic at the idea of having to take care of another human being or her worry at not doing a good job.

"You know, I can almost hear you thinking," Dallas whispered.

"Sorry," Viv murmured back. "I thought you were sleeping."

"I dozed off," Dallas admitted. "But, I can't sleep with these two in the bed with me. I never was much of a co-sleeping parent. I always worried I'd roll over on the baby and smush her." Viv watched as Dallas shimmied down the bed, trying to escape her sleeping children. Viv softly giggled and Dallas shot her a look that she was less amused by the whole scene.

"What's up?" Dallas asked.

"It's more like what's out," Viv corrected. She framed her growing belly with her hands, stretching Cillian's t-shirt over her expanding waist.

Now it was Dallas' turn to laugh. "Yeah, I'd love to tell you it gets better but it doesn't. It gets worse, Viv. So much worse. I wish I could help you out but I don't have any maternity clothes here."

"I figured. Can you help me convince the guys to get me some? I'm pretty sure that they'll think I just want to go on a shopping spree but I feel like I can't breathe in any of my clothes. It's getting to the point where I just want to walk around naked."

"Lead with that," Dallas offered. "Tell Cillian that you'll prance around naked and he'll take you out shopping."

"I do not prance," Viv protested. "But, I see your point. That might just work."

"I'll back you, Viv. Just say the word and I'll push Savage and Bowie to support you," Dallas promised.

"You just don't want me walking around naked in front of your guys," Viv grumbled.

Dallas giggled and nodded. "True," she admitted. "But, I also remember just how miserable it was at the stage you're in. You can't fit in any of your clothes and you just want to cry and eat ice cream. Am I right?"

"Yeah," Viv sighed. "Exchange ice cream with cookies and you have me pegged."

"What if we persuade the guys to let you shop online and have everything delivered? That way you wouldn't go out, putting yourself in danger. I could help you pick some stuff out," Dallas offered.

"I'd appreciate that, Dallas." Viv turned to leave the room. "And, if that suggestion fails, I can still walk around naked to solve my problem."

Cillian walked into Dallas' room, as if on cue. "Here you are," he said. "I was starting to worry that you snuck out. Everything all right?" He looked past Dallas and Viv to where the kids were napping and smiled. "They're so cute when they sleep," he said.

Dallas barked out her laugh, "So, what are they when they are awake?" she teased. Cillian looked a little flustered, causing them both to giggle. "Don't look so serious Cillian," she said. "I was just teasing you."

Cillian blew out his breath and chuckled. "So, what are you two up to, you know, besides busting my balls?"

"Well," Dallas said, looking over at Viv. "Your baby is growing like a weed and Viv needs some clothes that fit her." Dallas patted Viv's belly for good measure.

"I get it," Cillian said. "I can't let you go off on a shopping spree right now. It's just not safe." Viv could feel herself pout and she knew she wasn't playing fair. "Don't give me the bottom lip, Viv. You know it's just not right to go out now. We don't know where Dante is. He could be close and I won't risk you or our baby." He cupped her tummy and she swooned. Viv hated that she sometimes had the reactions to Cillian she had. It would be so much easier if she was able to stay mad at the man, but that was nearly impossible.

"I guess you are going to have to go with plan B," Dallas offered.

"What's plan B?" Cillian asked.

"She's going to prance around naked," Dallas said.

"I told you I don't prance," Viv huffed. "But she's not wrong. I'm running out of options here, Cillian," She said.

Cillian looked her up and down and nodded. "Fine," he agreed. "You and I go out alone and you don't leave my fecking side. We'll have Repo follow behind but keep his distance, just in case we have a tail. You will have one hour, at one store. Deal?"

"Yes," Viv squealed. Greer stirred on the bed and they collectively held their breaths, watching as the toddler settled back down to sleep. "Sorry," Viv breathed.

"That was a close one," Cillian agreed.

Dallas giggled, "You two have no idea. That was nothing—just wait, you'll see." Viv and Cillian groaned in unison and the baby woke up crying.

"Shit, sorry," Cillian grumbled. "How about we head out to get what you need and leave Dallas here to get some rest."

"That ship has sailed," Dallas mumbled. "But, go get Viv what she needs. Send Savage and Bowie back—they can take a turn with these two so I can grab a shower," she said. "Mama needs a break."

# CILLIAN

Repo agreed to shadow them for their little shopping trip and having him tag along made Kill feel a little more at ease about the whole situation. Honestly, he hated having to leave the safety of Repo's cabin and possibly put Viv and the baby at risk, but she was determined to get some clothes that fit. He wasn't opposed to the whole keeping her naked idea but in a houseful of people, that might not work out so well.

The got to the mall just as it opened and he looked at his watch. "You have about an hour, Love. Let's make this fast. Where to first?" he asked. Viv looked like a kid in a candy store the way she eyed all the stores.

"I read online that they have three stores for expectant moms," she gushed. "I even downloaded the map for the mall on my phone." She showed it to Kill and he couldn't help but feel her infectious excitement. It was nice to be out of the house. "I think we are here," she said, pointing to the phone screen.

"Yeah," Kill agreed. "Looks like the closest maternity store is this way." He grabbed her hand and started in the right direction. They quickly found the store and the sales clerk looked up and smiled, eyeing Viv's bump.

"Looks like you're ready for some new maternity clothing," the woman said. Viv covered her belly with her hands and giggled.

"Yeah," she agreed. "We're kind of bursting at the seams now." The woman smiled and nodded.

"If you'd like some help, just let me know," the woman said.

"That would be great," Viv agreed. "I know you want to keep a lookout," Viv whispered to Kill. "I'll be fine and I promise to hurry."

Kill kissed the top of her head. "I'll be just out front," he promised. "Yell if you need me." Kill walked out of the small store and looked over the very empty mall. He didn't believe that Dante would show up there, of all places, but he wouldn't take chances. Kill pulled his cell phone out to text Repo, wanting to find out where he was. Repo immediately responded that he was sitting in the parking lot watching their truck and keeping an eye out. Kill texted his thanks and peeked in on Viv. She was handing the sales lady items faster than the poor woman could put them in the dressing room for her and he laughed. His woman was a force.

By the time Viv had tried on half the store, Kill was starting to get antsy. His phone rang and he recognized Savage's number. "Hey man, everything okay?" Cillian asked.

"Yep," Savage said. "Sorry, maybe I should have texted first. I didn't mean to worry you. How's your shopping trip going?"

Kill smiled. "I had no idea women could shop so much. Viv gives new meaning to 'shop til you drop'," Kill said. Savage chuckled into the other end.

"Listen, man," Savage said. "The guys and I have done a little something for you and Viv and I don't want you to give me any shit about it." Cillian knew he wasn't going to like what Savage was going to say just by his tone.

"What did you do?" Kill asked. He sounded more like he was accusing his friend of something.

"We got you and Viv a little pre-wedding gift," Savage said. "At least, that's what Dallas told me to call it. I know things are tough and we wanted to help. So, I've contacted the jewelry store on the second floor of the mall. Go there and they'll explain the rest."

"I'm not going to like this, am I, man?" Cillian asked. He hated handouts and Savage had done enough hand-holding and supporting him, to last a lifetime. Kill knew that telling his friend no wouldn't do him any good. When Savage was determined to do something, no one stood in his way. Savage had taken Kill on as his little pet project and there would be no stopping him.

"Whatever it is, I'm going to pay you back," Kill insisted when Savage didn't answer him.

"No," Savage barked. "You won't. You're just going to have to accept that you're family now, Cillian. I have something else I want to talk to you about privately, but it can wait until things calm down. Helping you is just going to happen man—like it or not, Cillian. You saved my daughter. I owe you everything and I plan on following through."

Viv came bouncing out of the store, holding a bunch of bags. He took them from her. "Who's on the phone?" she asked.

"Savage," Kill said. "He wants us to run a little errand for him. You good?" Viv nodded.

"Hungry but good," she agreed.

Cillian laughed, "I'll do what you asked and then I think I need to feed my woman. We'll be back soon and you and I are going to have a little chat, Savage. You might think you owe me but that's just not true." He ended the call before Savage could get another word in, knowing he'd pay for that later.

"Let's go," Viv said. She wrapped her arm around his. "The sooner we run Savage's errand, the sooner I can eat."

---

"You want to say that again?" Kill asked the young, pasty salesclerk who was trying to explain to him that the guys at Savage Heat along with Savage had paid for wedding bands for him and Viv.

The poor guy looked about ready to run to the backroom to hide. "How about you go easy on him, Cillian?" Viv asked. Putting her hand on his arm. "He's just the messenger. Your friends are trying to do something nice for you—for us."

"Right," Cillian growled. "But, it feels like a handout. I can do this kind of shit on my own." He would too, someday. Right now, he was busy getting his life back and every cent he made went into his account to save for the shop he planned on opening. Kill paid his way and he found that he didn't need much. He was able to put most of his paycheck in the bank but at the rate he was going, it was going to take him forever to get to the point of realizing his dream.

The whole time he was behind bars, he dreamt of opening a garage. He had earned his mechanic's certificate while he was away and honestly, a day spent under the hood of a car was a pretty fucking fantastic day. He just wished he could get to the point of being able to afford all the things in life he wanted. All the stuff he wanted to give to Viv and now their baby.

"I understand that, Love," Kill almost whispered. He pulled her against his body and wrapped his arms around her. "I just wanted to do this for you. Savage has already done so much for me."

"He loves you, Cillian. Savage considers you a brother and I'm sure that if you refuse this, you'll insult him and the other guys. I, for one, think this is a perfect wedding gift. We don't need a toaster or dishes. I already had all that stuff. Wedding bands are very meaningful. It's a symbol of our lives together," she said.

"Well shit," Cillian grumbled. "When you say stuff like that, how can I stay mad?"

"You can't," Viv teased. "I'm pretty irresistible and very persuasive when I want to be."

Cillian chuckled, "That's true, Love. How about you look around and find what you want and I'll stop yelling at poor—" Kill stared down the salesclerk and when he made no move to give his name, Viv giggled.

"I think what my fiancé is trying to say is that he's sorry and he'd like to know your name."

"Oh—well, it's John," the salesclerk admitted.

"Okay, John," Kill said. "Let's find my woman a ring and I promise not to yell at you anymore—deal?" John nodded his agreement and led the way over to the case that held the wedding bands.

"They are all so beautiful," Viv gushed. Watching her weigh her options was pretty damn cute. Kill liked the way she bit her bottom lip into her mouth every time she asked the salesclerk to pull one from the case. She'd look at how much the band cost, make a face and then slip it onto her finger. Kill could tell as soon as she found the one she loved and when she told John to stick it back in the case, the kid looked at her just as baffled as Kill felt.

"Wait a minute," Kill protested. "You love that one, don't you?"

"Cillian, it's too expensive," she protested. "It doesn't leave much money for your band. We should split the gift. I won't hog it." Kill rolled his eyes and smiled.

"John," he said. "We'll take that one and—" he looked over the men's bands and pointed to a black one that had caught his eye earlier. It was plain and probably didn't cost very much. It was perfect for him. He'd be able to wear it to work, even when he was stuck under the hood of a car, elbow deep in oil and dirt.

"That one," Kill said, pointing to the band he wanted.

"No, Cillian," Viv protested.

"It's what I want, Viv. I've told you that someday, I'd like to open a garage," he said. Viv nodded.

"Sure," she said. "What does that have to do with choosing a wedding band though?"

"This material is perfect for a man who works with his hands—especially dirt and grease," John piped up.

"What he said," Kill agreed. "It's perfect for me—just like you're perfect for me, Viv."

"Okay, now you're just saying shit to butter me up and get me to agree with whatever you want," Viv complained.

"Is it working?" Kill asked.

Viv giggled and nodded. "Yeah," she admitted.

"Great," Kill breathed. "Wrap them both up for us, John. I've promised my woman some food and then we have to finish shopping. We're running out of time, Honey. The last thing either of us wants is for Savage to send out a search party."

"No," Viv said. "Thanks, Cillian," she said, going up on her tiptoes to kiss him. "I'm not sure how I got so lucky finding you," she said.

"Well, Lucky is my middle name," he teased. At least, he felt lucky as hell for having Viv in his life.

# VIVIAN

They ate lunch and Cillian allowed her to go to two more stores before he decided to end their day. They were walking back to the rental truck when pain ripped through her abdomen, causing her to drop the bag she was carrying, doubling over to hold her belly.

"Viv," Cillian shouted, rushing to her side. He dropped the bags to the ground and pulled her into his arms, cradling her against his body. "Tell me what's wrong," he insisted.

"It's the baby," she cried. "I think something's wrong."

"Don't panic, Love," Cillian said. "I've got you."

"I think we need to go to the hospital," she said.

Repo pulled up beside them in his pick-up and cut the engine. "What's wrong?" he asked.

"Viv's having pains," Cillian said. "I need to take her to be checked at the hospital." He looked around the parking lot at the scattered shopping bags.

"Don't worry about anything but your girl," Repo said. "I've got all this and will meet you over at the hospital.

It's one of the best, Kill. Don't worry, Viv will be in good hands."

"Thanks, man," Cillian said. Viv's abdomen cramped and she cried out. "Shit—call the others for us."

"Will do," Repo agreed. "Just get her to the hospital."

Cillian slid her into the passenger seat and buckled her in. Viv felt a fresh wave of panic wash over her as another sharp cramping sensation felt like it knotted up her insides. She doubled over and groaned, clutching her belly.

"Shit," Cillian spat. "I'll have you to the hospital in just a few tics, Love," he promised. Viv knew that something had to be wrong. If she had to guess, she was in labor and it was too soon.

"I'm just five months," she whispered. "It's too soon."

"No," Cillian said. "Don't think like that, Viv. The baby will be fine. We just need to have you both checked out." Viv knew he was trying to make her feel better but she wanted to tell Cillian he was wrong. She wanted to tell him not to make her false promises and give her hope because that wasn't usually how the world worked. At least, not for her.

Cillian had them to the hospital in record time and pulled up to the ER, not bothering with finding a parking spot. Two women rushed out of the building with a gurney and helped her from the truck and up onto the bed. "She's five months pregnant and we think she's having contractions," Cillian said. "She keeps having pains in her stomach."

"It feels like sharp pains, almost like my muscles and skin are being stretched," Viv added.

"Have you timed them?" the woman Viv assumed to be the nurse asked.

"No," Viv admitted. "I didn't know I needed to."

"That's okay," the woman said. "We'll get you in and hooked up to a machine that will be able to tell us if you are contracting and how far apart they are. We'll also get an ultrasound to check on your little one. You're in good hands." Viv nodded, not able to speak past the lump of emotion in her throat.

"We got this, Love. Our babe will be just fine—promise," Cillian said.

"Don't make me promises that might not be true," Viv whispered.

"How are you two related?" the second woman asked.

"I'm her fiancé and the baby's father," Cillian said. "Where she goes I go." He looked about as mean as they came and when he stared down the poor nurse Viv wanted to laugh. But, none of this was funny.

"You alright with this, Ma'am?" the first woman asked.

"Yes," Viv said. "I need him with me. Just find out what's wrong and fix it, please," she begged.

---

They got her hooked up to a machine that could measure if she was having contractions and the nurse said that the steady lines that the machine was producing, was a good sign. It felt like it took forever for a doctor to see her and after he checked her out, he left the room, not offering any explanation. Viv couldn't help her worry. She felt consumed by it and when she started to cry, Cillian was by her side, holding her hand.

"Whatever it is, Love, we'll get through it—together," he promised.

"This is all my fault," she sobbed. "I wasn't sure I wanted this baby and now, we might not have him or her. I did this." When she found out she was pregnant Viv thought about having an abortion. Hell, she had only just met Cillian and they were so new to each other. Viv didn't expect him to stick around when she told him about the baby and she wasn't sure she'd be able to raise a kid on her own. But then, she thought about what her grandmother would say about the baby being a blessing and how they bring so much joy to a family—it was almost impossible to follow through with her initial plans. Viv decided to keep the baby and tell Cillian, letting the chips fall where they may. It had all worked out—she got the man she loved and a baby she was falling more and more in love with each passing day. If something happened to the baby, she'd be the one to blame.

"Viv," Cillian whispered, pulling her close. The door opened again and a guy pushed a cart into the room with some sort of machine on it.

"Miss Ward?" he questioned.

"Yes." She sniffled. "I'm Vivian Ward."

"I'm an ultrasound technician and I'll be doing you're sonogram today. Ready to see your baby?" he asked.

Viv nodded and sobbed, "Yes. Will you be able to tell us if the baby is alright?"

"I'm going to do my best," he promised. Viv let him raise the hospital gown she had put on and watched as he squirted a warm gel onto her lower abdomen. "This won't hurt at all, Miss Ward," he promised. He pushed a small wand over her skin and rolled it over her belly; an image appearing as soon as he did.

"Is that the baby?" Cillian asked.

"Yes," the technician said. He continued to work the wand over her belly, taking measurements and taking pictures of the baby as he went. "This is a 4D sonogram and it will give us clear pictures of your baby. Here is her heart and it looks strong. I'm going to ask you to be still for just a moment, so I can get a measure of her heartbeats per minute." Viv did as he asked, even holding her breath to make sure she was completely still.

"Is the baby alright?" Cillian asked.

The tech nodded, "Her heartbeat is strong. I'll print out some pictures for you to take with you."

"You keep calling the baby a 'she'," Viv said. "Are we having a girl?"

"I'm sorry," the technician said. "Were you not going to find out the sex?"

She looked at Cillian and he shrugged and nodded. "It looks like we're having a girl," he said. He smiled at the sonogram screen, seeming almost hypnotized by the tiny form moving inside of Viv's belly.

Viv wiped at her tears as they fell down her cheeks. "Is she alright?" she asked. "I mean, does she look healthy?"

The technician nodded, "She looks great." He printed off some pictures and handed them to Viv. She looked at her daughter's face, able to see her perfect little features.

"She looks just like you," Viv whispered to Cillian. "She's so beautiful." The technician wiped the extra gel from Viv's belly and pulled her gown back down.

"The doctor will be in to talk to you in a few minutes, but I believe you're going to be just fine," the technician promised. "Good luck with your little one."

"Thank you," Viv said, still studying the pictures. "For everything." The tech left the tiny ER room and Cillian sat down next to her on the gurney.

"A girl," he whispered, taking the pictures from her. "We have a daughter."

The doctor walked into the room and smiled at them, "Looks like you are clear to go back home," he said. Viv wished that was true. She wanted more than anything to be able to return to Huntsville and her little diner. She had so much to do before their daughter made her way into the world and seeing her today made that all too clear.

"What were the pains?" Viv asked. "Were they contractions?"

"No," the doctor said. "The uterus expands quickly at this point in your pregnancy. You will experience pains like that as your baby continues to grow. It's like stretching a rubber band and your skin and muscles have to adapt. Sometimes women have pain and other times, nothing. You are just one of the unlucky ones who will experience the burning and stretching sensations of the baby growing."

"So, we aren't in any danger?" Viv asked.

"Nope," the doctor said.

"It wouldn't hurt you to drink more water." He handed her a reusable water bottle and smiled. "Eight of these a day."

"I'll be living in the bathroom," she grumbled.

"You have no idea," the doctor said. "My wife had our first baby last year and she practically spent the whole last trimester in the bathroom. Are you taking prenatal vitamins?" he asked.

"No," Viv said. "I was only able to visit the doctor to confirm the pregnancy and then life got a little turned upside down."

"Well, I want you to pick some up today and start taking them. They will help with overall health, for you and the baby, as well as your energy levels. Follow up with your OBGYN in about two weeks, or sooner if the pains persist." Viv and Cillian thanked the doctor and she got dressed.

"I guess we will need to find a doctor around here," Viv whispered.

"Let me talk to Savage and I'll work it all out, Love. You just worry about taking care of you and the baby," Cillian said.

---

Viv could feel the tension as soon as she walked through the door to Repo's cabin. Cillian and Repo seemed to sense it too, going on high alert before they found everyone in the kitchen. "What's wrong?" Cillian asked as soon as he saw Savage.

Savage looked at Viv and smiled, "How did it go at the ER? What did the doctor say?"

Viv knew he was changing the subject, trying to avoid Cillian's question but she decided to play along. "The doctor said I was just experiencing growing pains and that we are having a girl."

"Oh my gosh," Dallas gushed. "Congratulations you two." Dallas stood and handed Greer to Bowie, crossing the room to pull Viv in for a quick hug. "Don't worry about the growing pains," she said. "I had them with Greer too."

"Thanks," Viv said. "I think I'll be asking you for advice when it comes to this pregnancy stuff. Ignoring the growing human inside of me won't work for very much longer." Dallas giggled. "Oh, and if you could recommend a good prenatal vitamin, that would be great."

"We will need to find a good OBGYN in the area," Cillian added. "Viv needs to see the doctor again in two weeks."

"Well, that might not be an issue," Savage said. Maybe you should sit for this next part, Viv," he added.

"Why," she asked. "What's happened. Dallas took her over to the big dining table and pulled out a chair next to her own.

"It's good news," Bowie said. Cillian stood at her back and she could feel the tension coming from him. He put his hand on her shoulder and she reached up and covered it with her own.

"Dante's dead," Savage said.

"How can you be sure?" Cillian asked. Viv wanted to celebrate and be excited about the news but how could they be sure that they were safe? What if this was all a sick ploy to get them to return home to Huntsville?

Hart sat forward, "I can confirm the news," he promised. "Dante's dead and from the intel I got, it was one of his men who did the deed."

"Shit," Cillian growled. "How can we be sure it's safe to go home?"

"We can't be positive that it will ever be safe, Kill," Repo said. "We just have to trust Hart's intel and hope for the best. I'm ready to have you people out of my cabin," he teased. Viv could tell that Repo was trying to make lite of the situation but the worry she saw in the other guy's eyes told her a different story. They were all worried about returning home.

"I'd like to go home," Viv almost whispered. "I really would like to see my OBGYN, just to make sure everything is all right with the baby."

"I can run you and Kill back to Huntsville, so you can see your doctor, Viv," Ryder offered. "Then, I can do a little recon to make sure that the story of Dante's death is on the up and up. If everything checks out, I can swing back over here and pick-up the rest of you," he said.

Savage looked between Bowie and Dallas and they seemed to do a whole silent communication thing. Viv had been watching the three of them together for a few weeks now and she had to admit, at first she wondered how three people in a relationship could work. But, seeing how well the three of them managed their little family, changed her mind. They not only worked well together; they were the most functional family unit she had ever witnessed. She just hoped that she and Cillian had their shit together even one-tenth as much as the three of them seemed to.

"Fine," Savage said. "How about if the two of you talk this through, Cillian. It's a big decision to make. If you go back to Huntsville and Dante is still alive, that could mean trouble for you and Viv. Be sure."

Viv stood and yawned, "Can we hash this out later, Cillian? I'm exhausted from our day. Thank you—all of you—for our wedding present. I can't tell you how special it was to us both that you'd want to do that for us." Cillian reached for her hand and smiled.

"Thanks, guys," he said. "Viv convinced me that you did it because you care and she's right, we appreciate it. We can't wait to start our lives together as husband and wife and we're damn lucky to have friends like the lot of you."

"Your family, Cillian," Savage said. "You and Viv both are now. We take care of our own, man." Viv had to admit that being a part of a family again, even their mishmash MC crew felt right. Cillian was right—they were pretty damn lucky.

# CILLIAN

Kill tossed and turned for a half hour and he decided to finally give in to his grumbly stomach and go in search of something to eat. He quietly slipped from the bed, careful not to wake Viv. She was exhausted and needed her rest, especially if he was going to keep his promise and take her back to Huntsville in the morning.

He bumped into Savage in the hallway and he followed Kill into the kitchen. It was the middle of the night and neither wanted to wake any of the others. "How's Viv?" he asked.

Cillian smiled and nodded, "She's sleeping. I told her we can head back home in the morning and she's beyond excited. I know it's a bit of a risk, but I also trust Hart. If he says Dante's dead, I believe him. Why aren't you sleeping?"

"I heard you wandering around out here and I wanted to check in and make sure everything is good. Viv hasn't had any more pain?" Savage asked.

"Sorry I woke you," Cillian said. "And, Viv and the baby are both fine. She just gave her mom and me a little scare."

"I still can't believe you're having a little girl, man?" Savage said, grinning like a complete fool.

"Yep," Cillian said. "I can hardly believe it myself. If you would have told me just a year ago, that I was going to meet the woman of my dreams and we'd be having a little girl, I would have told you that you were crazy."

"Well, Bowie, Dallas and I are happy for you. Chloe wants to know if she can help name the baby," Savage said rolling his eyes.

Kill chuckled, "No—she can't. Thanks, Savage," Kill said. He honestly hadn't been able to stop smiling since they saw their little girl on the ultrasound. "I'm going to make myself a midnight snack. Want to join?" Savage nodded and followed Kill to the kitchen.

Hart stormed into the kitchen and Cillian felt bad that they had woken him. Judging from the look on Hart's face, Kill knew he wasn't going to like a word that he was going to say. "Someone want to tell me what the fuck this is?" Hart barked. He held up a tiny piece of metal and Kill knew exactly what it was.

"Bug," Kill breathed. "Where the fuck did you find it?"

"In my fucking room," Hart shouted.

Repo and Ryder joined them in the kitchen, both yawning and rubbing the sleep from their eyes. Kill's little midnight snack was turning into one huge mess. "I put it there," Repo admitted.

"What the fuck, man?" Hart yelled. "What for?"

"To make sure you were on the up and up, man. You're not a part of Savage Hell and we don't know if we can trust you," Repo admitted.

Hart pointed an accusing finger in Cillian's direction and Savage growled. "He's not a member of Savage Hell either. You put a bug in his fucking room?" he asked.

"Keep your voice down, Hart. If you wake up my kids, my wife will have my balls. And for the record, just because Cillian's not a patched member doesn't mean he's not a part of our club, asshole" Savage said. "I've known Cillian longer than I've known anyone else here. He's good. You, on the other hand, are new here. I told Repo to put that bug in your room. You have a problem with it, you come to me," he said. Hart stood toe to toe with Savage and Kill was sure he was going to have to intervene.

"I have a fucking problem with it," Hart grumbled. "And, I'm officially letting you know."

"Fair enough, Hart," Savage said. "I will round up the rest."

"Rest of what?" Hart asked. "Bugs? You fucker," he spat. "There are more?"

Savage's smile was mean, "Yep," he confirmed. "As I said, I'm protecting my own."

"You know, I have a mind not to tell you what I found out," Hart grumbled.

Cillian knew that Hart could be an asshole when he wanted to be. He hated that Hart would keep information they might need, to keep their families safe, and not share it. Savage growled, "You want to keep your fucking head attached to your shoulders, start talking," he said. The threat seemed to only make Hart want to stall more.

"I thought you agreed to be a part of this team," Repo said. "I know you're an outsider, Hart. We've all been at one point or another. Hell, it hasn't been that long since I was new to Savage Hell. We all just have to prove ourselves—you included. Too much is at stake not to speak up. They had little Chloe—we can't let that happen again," Repo whispered.

Hart sighed and nodded. "You're right. I won't let them take another little girl. My guy on the inside got a message to me. The Dragons have a new Prez," Hart said.

"What does that mean for the human trafficking business they were running?" Cillian asked.

"It means that we can all safely go home," Hart said.

"How can you be sure we'll be safe?" Savage asked. "Do you know who the new Prez is?"

"Yeah," Hart admitted. "You didn't hear this from me, but I think the guy can be trusted."

"And, we're supposed to just take your word for this? We're talking about the safety of our families," Savage challenged. "I won't base their safety on a feeling, Hart."

"It's more than that," Hart admitted. "Shit, I can't tell you this but their new Prez, Outkast, is my inside guy. He's been deep undercover for years now. If word got out, he'd be killed."

"Fuck," Cillian cursed.

"I know Outkast," Savage admitted. "I had no fucking idea he was working for the cops."

"This whole thing has to stay between us. He's been working to bring down that trafficking ring for a while now. If you blow is cover, all that work will be lost," Hart said.

"You have my word," Savage said. "Outkast's secret is safe with all of us. Right guys?" Repo, Ryder, and Cillian nodded their agreement. "Just let us know what we can do to help out. Name it, and it's done."

"I appreciate that, Savage," Hart said. "There is something I need. We need to keep up appearances and one of the things that will need to happen is Outkast will need to meet with you—Prez to Prez."

"Yeah," Savage said. "That's the way it usually works. One club will invite the other over and either declare war or ask for peace. Which will Outkast want between the Dragons and Savage Hell?"

"Peace," Hart said. "He'll need that to focus on the group's business. He'll put on a show, but he'll agree to peace."

"I guess we all go home in the morning," Savage said. "Can you have the plane ready, Ryder?"

"Yep. I was ready to fly Viv and Savage back. I'll adjust the passenger list in the morning when I turn in our flight plan."

"That works. Let's be ready to roll out by ten," Savage ordered. They agreed and Kill had to admit it felt damn good to be heading home. As far as he was concerned, this shit storm with the Dragons couldn't end soon enough.

---

They had only been home for a day and a half before Savage Hell was summoned to the Dragon's bar. Kill had barely enough time to catch his damn breath before the meeting was set up and when Savage asked him to have his six, he immediately agreed. What else could he do but tell Savage yes after the guy had saved his ass on more than one occasion?

Viv was glad to be back home and she was even gearing up to re-open the diner in a few days. Kill worried that she was taking on too much but she went to see her doctor, just to confirm the diagnosis they got in the ER, and she had the all-clear to return to work. She promised to rest and let others do the heavy lifting, but he knew his Viv and she was as stubborn as the day was long.

"You ready to do this?" Savage asked. They were sitting in his pickup and neither made a move to get out of the truck.

Kill shrugged, "As I'll ever be," he breathed. "It's just weird being back here and I'm worried we'll say something to blow Outkast's cover. I don't want to fuck this up," he admitted.

"So, don't," Savage said. "Let's just get in and have this damn meeting and get this shit show over with." Kill and Savage walked into the Dragon's bar and he pushed down the moment of panic he experienced being back in that hell hole. He could still taste the blood from his busted lip every time he thought back to that night just weeks prior. The smell of urine in the basement, from the cages that lined the walls, still made him feel nauseous. The cages that he knew held those poor women awaiting their fate to be sold off to the highest bidder. But, they weren't there under the same circumstances this time—at least that was what he was telling himself. Dante's reign was over and Kill had to remember that despite the way things appeared, their new Prez—Outkast, was on their side. They just needed to keep their heads for this little meeting and not blow the guy's cover. This meeting was just a formality and then their families would be safe—at least that was the plan. Kill knew that was what Savage was hoping for and he felt the same. He couldn't settle for anything less, not with Viv and a baby girl on the way. He wouldn't let anyone threaten his family again—ever.

"Gentlemen," Outkast said, meeting them at the front door. He was flanked on either side by his enforcers. Kill choked back the bile that rose to his mouth at the sight of the two guys he had to take down during his time in the cage they kept in the basement. They still had the faded bruises and cuts from their fight. The big guy wore a sling on his left arm and he seemed just as upset to see Kill, although he had to give the guy credit—he didn't back down.

"Come on in and make yourself at home," Outkast offered, holding his arms wide. "Our bar is at your disposal. Can I get you a beer?"

"It's nine in the morning," Savage protested. Kill wanted to take the guy up on his offer. Hell, he could do with a shot of whiskey or two, but Savage was right. They needed to keep their heads straight if they were going to get through this little meeting.

"Of course," Outkast agreed. His smile was warm and Kill could tell the guy was trying for friendly, but it was a lie. His smile didn't reach his eyes and Kill knew that the Dragon's new Prez was putting on a show. Kill almost wished he wasn't privy to the news that Outkast was an undercover cop. Their meeting would be easier to get through if Kill could just hate the guy.

"Let's just get down to business," Savage challenged. "Why have we been summoned here, Outkast?"

"I've always liked your no-nonsense way of ruling Savage Hell, man," Outkast said. On the flight home, Savage filled the guys in on the research he had done on Outkast. He seemed to have a complete disregard for the rules, both written and implied. There was usually no room for someone like that in the MC world, but Outkast wasn't a part of that world. He was straddling the right side of evil and he had to make his own rules. Otherwise, he'd be discovered. Savage's MC world didn't work quite that way. Kill knew that his friend valued loyalty above all else and trust was king. Without those things, Savage Hell wouldn't exist.

"Funny," Savage spat. "Usually, when someone admires someone else, they don't stab them in the fucking back," he growled. Savage took a step towards Outkast and his enforcers blocked him with their bodies. Outkast had the poor judgment to find the whole scene funny and for just a minute, Kill was sure things were about to turn ugly. Savage was certainly playing his part in all this. Hell, maybe he was looking for someone to take his anger out on for taking Chloe. He still hadn't worked through all that and now, with Dante gone, Outkast was the next best person to pound his anger out on.

"Easy man," Kill warned. "This isn't why we are here, Savage."

"You should listen to your man, Savage," Outkast said. "He's not wrong."

"Fine, let's just get this over with," Savage ordered. Even when he wasn't in charge, Savage seemed to take the position of power. He was just one of those guys and Kill would follow him to hell and back.

"Okay," Outkast agreed. "I called you here to make sure that we understand each other, Savage."

"What's there to understand?" Savage asked. "Your club took my little girl and threatened our women. There's nothing to understand here, Outkast."

"This is on your club, really," Outcast said.

"How do you figure?" Savage barked.

"Cut off the serpent's head and two more grow in its place, Savage. Did you think that Dante was as high up as they run in the Dragons? Like your Savage Hell club is just a small piece of the Royal Bastards, the Dragons are a part of the Anarchy Kings. We answer to them and they make sure that everyone on our end is on the up and up. Dante wasn't, so they took care of him. Good news for you is, I don't have a problem with you, Savage. You keep your little gang out of my way and out of my fucking business and I'll leave Savage Hell alone. You good with that?"

Savage looked at Kill and God, he wanted to believe Outkast. All they wanted was to live in peace and that's what he was offering them. But, at what price? Kill knew what was waiting in the basement. Could they turn a blind eye to the fact that the Dragons were trafficking women and girls, just to save their own families?

Kill watched as Savage seemed to struggle with the same thoughts. Outkast held his hand out for Savage as if waiting for him to accept his deal. Savage didn't take it. "You can't believe you'll get away with it, right?" Savage asked. "Trafficking women and children won't be tolerated—not by Savage Hell." Jesus, Kill wanted to tell him to back down, but his friend was right. They couldn't allow something so evil to exist in their town. It wasn't who they were as men or as a club. The guys in the club weren't angels by any stretch of the imagination but they weren't evil assholes either. Trafficking women and children was just plain evil.

Outkast lowered his hand, his smile was mean. "Suit yourself, Savage. You can't say I didn't warn you. You come after my club or my business and we won't pull our punches. Is Savage Hell a sacrifice you're willing to make to bring down my little business? Is your family something either of you is willing to forfeit to bring down the Dragons?" Outcast challenged.

"We'll see," Savage shrugged. "If the Dragons keep their noses clean, we won't have a problem."

"I'm sorry that this meeting didn't go the way I was hoping for, Savage," Outkast said. "You can see yourselves out, I'm sure." Outkast turned his back on them and walked back to his office, leaving his two sentries to stand guard. Savage chuckled and turned to leave.

"This is over, Cillian. For now, at least," he added. Kill hated that they were leaving their meeting without resolving the issues, but he followed Savage's lead. He smiled at the two goons staring him down, even winking at them before turning to walk out the front door. Kill had a sick feeling that wouldn't be his last run-in with the Dragon's enforcers, but that would be a fight for another day. For now, he'd have to settle for the promise of tomorrow with Viv as his wife. He was going to meet his woman at the courthouse and make her his, officially.

"Well, that was a shit show," Kill grumbled. "I have to give it to Outkast, he was pretty damn convincing. You think that was all for show or what?"

"I have no idea, man," Savage admitted. "I guess we only have Hart's word to go by and well, time. If Outkast is one of the good guys, we'll know sooner or later."

"So we wait?" Kill asked.

"Yeah besides, we have bigger things to think about today. You ready for this?" Savage asked.

"If you mean marrying the woman I want more than my next breath—then yeah," Kill admitted. "I think I've been waiting my whole life for Viv."

"Then let's go and get you hitched," Savage said, patting Kill's shoulder. "We'll worry about all this other shit another day." Kill nodded and smiled, knowing his friend was right. The rest of the crap could wait. Today, he was going to begin his forever with his woman and that was enough for him.

---

Cillian stood at the front of the courtroom and wanted to laugh at how different things were from the first time he was in that same room. Last time, he was being sentenced by a judge for grand theft auto. This time, he was going to be professing his undying love for Viv, in front of the justice of the peace, making her his wife. Viv walked down the short span of the aisle, wearing a beautiful white lacey dress she borrowed from Dallas. It was the same dress she had worn for her commitment ceremony with Bowie and Savage. Kill loved the sweet friendship that was forming between his and Savage's woman. It was fitting that their two families would be close. Kill could see their kids growing up together, family birthday parties and even vacations. He wondered how his parents would feel about the way things had turned out for him. Kill knew his father trusted Savage with his own life, time and again. He had to believe both of his parents would approve of him leaning on Savage and offering him his friendship. It was what his father had asked of Savage before heading back to Ireland; him keeping an eye on Kill. Now, it was his turn to help Savage keep an eye on the people he loved and his club. It was the least Kill could do for his old friend after he stood by him for so many years.

"Hi," Viv said, smiling up at him. She carried a small bouquet of lilies and she looked perfect. Her long blond hair laid in soft curls on her bare shoulders and the dress hugged her every curve, even the baby bump that Kill was fascinated with. He never thought that any of this would be possible for him—a wife and kids, but here he was with everything he'd ever wanted in life.

"Hey," he whispered, pulling her against his body to brush his lips against hers. The judge cleared his throat and the two of them laughed. "Sorry," he lied.

"You look beautiful," she whispered. Kill looked down his own body and smiled. He was wearing the blue suit that Dallas had bought for him when he got out of prison. It was supposed to be for job interviews, but he never needed it. He found a job that led him to his happily ever after—his forever.

"Right back at you," he whispered. "You look lovely, Viv," Cillian said. Her blush was adorable, reaching up to her ears and Kill wondered how he had gotten so damn lucky in finding Viv. "Thank you for agreeing to marry me," he said, taking her hand in his own.

"Thanks for asking, Cillian," she whispered.

"Are you both ready to begin?" the judge asked.

"We are," they said together. Their beginning was just the start of what Kill wanted to build with his new wife. He could tell by the way she looked at him, Viv felt the same way. He was ready for today and every day after because of the promise he saw in her eyes. Viv was his home and he'd finally found his way to her. Cillian was exactly where he was supposed to be—home.

## EPILOGUE

# VIVIAN

It had been one year since Cillian James walked into her life. Viv's life changed forever that day. It was the day she hired the hot as sin ex-con, covered in tattoos and able to melt her panties with just one word in his sexy Irish accent. Yeah, Cillian was a nice surprise and just when she thought life couldn't take her by surprise anymore, the universe sent her their baby girl.

Viv looked down at her sleeping two-month-old daughter and sighed. Little Jessica was the spitting image of her father and she had him completely wrapped around her tiny finger. They debated on the name until one night when they were at Savage Hell and one of the guys in the club said they should name the baby Jesse James, like the outlaw. Cillian was immediately on board but she worried that the name was too masculine. Cillian came up with Jessica and she agreed to let him call her Jesse, for short. She had to admit, knowing her daughter's short temperament and hot head, the name seemed to fit her.

"Let's go on a little walk, Jesse. I think your Daddy is going to work late tonight and we'll bring him some dinner," Viv whispered, kissing her daughter's fuzzy little head.

Viv had hired a full-time manager at the diner to keep up the place. She still went in every morning but was home in time for Cillian to go into his shop by lunchtime, most days. They had a great little system worked out and were lucky enough to both be business owners, allowing them time with Jesse. While she was still pregnant, Viv worried that their schedules might be too much on their growing family, but it seemed to work for them.

The guys at Savage Hell had decided to give Cillian a loan to start his shop. It had been his dream to open a garage in town and Savage even helped him to find the perfect location. The place had been a garage back in the day and it just took a little bit of elbow grease and the guys all pitched in to help get it up and running. It was so special to watch Cillian's dreams realized. She remembered what it was like her first day on the job as the owner of her grandmother's diner and not just an employee. She knew that the garage meant everything to Cillian and she was so proud of him. He called his place Roadkill and she had to admit, she loved the name. It seemed to fit both who Cillian was and the man he had become.

He had even made enough in the first few months to pay back most of his loan to Savage Hell. Savage had told him not to rush, but her husband didn't like to be in debt to anyone, not even men he considered family. They had decided to save everything he made from the shop until he could pay the club back, living off what she could bring home from the diner. Things were tight, but they were doing it. In just a few more months, Cillian would have his debt paid and own his garage free and clear.

Cillian worked on the club's vehicles at a discount and the guys gave him enough business to keep his place going for a good long time. Cillian hated taking money from the guys, after everything they had done for him, but Savage insisted that was the way it was going to be. Word got around town that he was not only a damn good mechanic, but trustworthy and charged a fair price, and people started taking their vehicles to him.

Viv put Jesse in her stroller and walked the mile to Cillian's garage, to take him the food she had brought home from the diner. "Well, there are my two best girls," he said, as they turned the corner. "What brings you in tonight?" he asked. He pulled Viv in for a quick kiss and peeked in on the sleeping baby.

"We missed you," Viv offered. "And, we thought you might want some dinner?"

"Well, I'm starving and I missed you both too. I'm almost ready to knock off for the night. You want to join me for supper?"

"I was hoping you'd ask," Viv said. "I brought dinner for two and I'm sure your daughter will wake up and fuss for her dinner soon enough."

"She's just like her mama," Cillian teased. "Fussy when she gets hungry."

"We call that 'hangry' in America," she said. Cillian chuckled and went to the back bathroom, to wash up.

"How about we eat in my office and you can both tell me about your day," he said.

"Well, I'm pretty sure Jesse won't have much of an update, but I got caught up on the mountain of laundry, so I'd count today as a win," Viv said. She sat down across from Cillian and he pulled food from the bag.

"I was going to come home and grab a quick bite, shower and head back out, but if you need me to stay home, I can," he offered. Viv knew he had church tonight over at Savage Hell. Tuesday nights were usually just her and Jesse curled up on the sofa, watching some reality television show. Viv knew how important church was to Cillian, especially since he was about to patch into the club. It was all he had ever wanted—to be a part of something and now, he was. She wouldn't take that from him.

"No, you go to church. Jesse and I will find something on television and try to wait up for you to get home. I won't make any promises about that last part though. Our little princess has been waking me up at four in the morning for her feeding, lately."

"You're sure?" Cillian asked.

"Yep. I'm hoping that sooner or later, I'll be able to go in with you and hang out with Dallas while you have your meeting. We've been wanting to get the kids together for a play date but Dallas said the baby had a cold and didn't want Jesse to catch it."

"Well, a playdate sounds like fun," Cillian said. "How about a Mommy and Daddy playdate this weekend?"

"What did you have in mind?" Viv asked. She had been to the doctor two days earlier and had been given the all-clear on the sex front. She knew that Cillian had been secretly marking off the days on his calendar that he kept in his desk, waiting for her to give him the green light.

"I was thinking a night away, just the two of us," he said.

Honestly, Viv wasn't sure she was ready to leave the baby, but she didn't want to turn down the opportunity to spend some one on one time with her husband. She knew how important that was for a newly married couple.

"You look a little worried," he said.

"I'm just not sure I'm ready to leave her," Viv admitted.

"I figured you would say that, so I took it upon myself to enlist some help." Cillian smiled across his desk at her, looking so damned pleased with himself.

"What did you do?" she questioned.

"Well, how about the three of us fly to Repo's cabin and stay for a few days. You know, get away from it all and reconnect?" Cillian bobbed his eyebrows at her for good measure, causing her to giggle.

"Now, how can I say no to an offer like that?" she asked.

"You can't," he confirmed. "We leave in two days—I've already worked it all out."

"Well, I guess that makes my answer a firm yes," she said.

"Happy one year anniversary, Love," Cillian said. Viv didn't realize he knew what today was until just now.

"You remembered?" she asked.

"How could I not?" Cillian questioned. "It's been the best year of my life. Thank you for giving me everything I've ever dreamed of and so much more that I had no clue I wanted." Cillian looked over to where Jesse slept in her stroller and smiled. He was right—together, they had built a life she never imagined possible. Cillian was that for her—dreams come true and possibilities imagined. He was her world and she wouldn't change a thing.

# CAT

Catrina Linz stood by the vending machine, handcuffs still on, waiting for her bail bondsman to show up. When she called the company she found in the ancient phone book, the guys baritone voice grumbled something about waking him up and getting him out of his warm bed. Cat wanted to point out that it was the middle of summer in Alabama and nearly a hundred degrees out. Everywhere was warm, so his argument didn't hold water, as her grandmother used to say. She just wanted to get home and wash away this whole fucking day and every one of the assholes who had used her body for their pleasure. Honestly, it had been a slow day. Fuck, if she was being completely honest, she'd admit that it had been a damn slow month. Cat wasn't sure how she was going to pay her rent and now, she was going to have to come up with the money to pay back her bail bondsman.

She slumped down into the chair next to the window. Maybe it was time to go back home and try to find some former semblance of her old life but that would mean she'd have to face her mother and her shitty step-father again. Hell, they'd probably insist that she admit she made the whole damn story up but she hadn't. He was the no-good disgusting fucker she claimed he was. He raped her, taking her virginity when she was only fourteen and told her that if she told her mother, he'd kill her and her little brother. Cat kept her fucking mouth shut and what did her good old stepdad do? He rewarded her by repeatedly raping her for the next two years. That was when she told her mother. The one person on the planet who should have had her back. The one woman who should have believed her and protected her but she hadn't. Instead, her mother accused her of being a slut and seducing her step-father. Her mom kicked her out and stayed with that douche and Cat's only regret was having to leave her little brother, Liam behind. He was four years younger than she was and she knew that dragging him with her would be no life for a kid. She was just a kid herself, but the world had taught her the hard way that sometimes, the only thing you can do is run. So, that's what she did. Cat ran and when she got tired of running, she ran some more. There wasn't any amount of distance that she could put between her and her step-father that would make her feel safe. She'd never feel that way again—safe, wanted, loved. Not that it mattered. Cat wasn't sure she had ever experienced any of those feelings in her short life—which sucked. Most women her age were married and had a kid or two. At twenty-seven, she decided that ship had left the harbor. Besides, who would want a woman as used up as she was?

"Cat Linz?" a very tall, tattooed guy looked her over and she squinted her eyes at him, trying to decide if she wanted to admit that he had the right person or send him packing. Honestly, the guy looked like one of her Johns and maybe he had been. With her luck, he was just some asshole who had paid her for sex. His smile was easy and God, he was good looking. Sure, it was in a surly hot biker kind of way, but if she had a type—this guy would fit it. That was one of the occupational hazards she faced though—every guy had to be her type or at least she had to pretend that was the case. His brown eyes were so dark, she was sure she could see her reflection in them and fuck, she looked like shit. He pushed his overly long brown hair back from his eyes and handed her a business card. She took it and tried to turn it over to read, but that feat felt impossible, given her constraints.

"You wanna help me out, here?" she asked, shoving the card back in his direction. The guy had the nerve to laugh and he took the card from her and turned it over, putting it back between her hands.

"Sorry," he said. "I'm Repo."

Now it was her turn to giggle, "As in like—you're repossessing a car?" she teased.

He shrugged, "Sure," he agreed. "But I repossess people. I'm your bail bondsman. Well, that is if you're Catrina Linz."

"Yeah," she breathed. "That's me. How much is this going to set me back?" she asked.

"Not much into small talk? I like that. I'm not either. Fifteen hundred. I pay up front and you pay me back. We can sign the papers when they process you for release. You don't pay me back on time—I find you. You run—"

"Let me guess, you find me?" she sassed. He rolled his eyes and nodded.

"This isn't something I take lightly. This is business," Repo spat.

"Fine," she said. "I agree. Just get me the fuck out of here." Repo called for one of the officers to help process her for release. This was only the third time she had been picked up for working the corner. How the hell was she supposed to know that the guy who picked her up tonight was a cop? Wasn't that entrapment or something? That was a question she'd ask her court-appointed lawyer because she certainly couldn't afford one. She just hoped that whoever got stuck with her case was willing to meet her on the street because that would be where she'd be living. Once she got back to her shithole apartment, she was pretty sure her landlord would be waiting for his rent. When she'd finally get around to telling him she doesn't have it again this month, he was going to toss her out on her ass. He had been threatening to do it for weeks now and she was out of time and excuses.

"Can we hurry this up? I have an apartment to be kicked out of and a street bench to claim?" Repo chuckled, as if she was kidding but none of this was a joke to her. The cop removed her cuffs and handed her a baggie full of her things.

Repo gave her the paperwork and a pen. "Read it over and if you have any questions, let me know." She smiled up at him and turned to the last page to fill out the personal information he required and signed her name on the line. She shoved the papers and pen back at him and he smiled at her. "Okay then," he said, taking the papers back from her. "Good doing business with you," he said. Cat watched as he turned the corner and then looked back.

"You were kidding about having to sleep on a bench, right? I mean, I'm only asking because I'll need an address to track you down in case you try to skip out on the cash I just put up for your ass." Repo didn't bother to walk back to where she was standing, just shouting his question for all the precinct to hear. Not that she cared. Cat stopped caring what other people thought about her a damn long time ago.

"I don't kid around a whole lot, Repo," she shouted back. "Business hasn't been that great and well, I don't have my rent. So yeah, I'm going to be evicted as soon as I get home. I'm betting my shit is already sitting by the curb, as we speak."

"Fuck," he cursed and walked back to her.

"I'm going to need an address or this won't work. You gave your friend Candy as your point of contact. Can you crash at her place?" She winced at his question. She sort of made that part up. She knew some woman named Candy but she had no idea where she lived. She was just some chick she some times passed the time with while they waited for their next clients. Candy was trying to get her to sign on with Sly—her pimp, but that wasn't something Cat wanted. She had always gone it alone and if she couldn't make it in Huntsville, Alabama, she'd find another place to run to because that's what she was good at.

# REPO

"Listen, how about we go out to the parking lot and you let me work off my debt with you and we can call it even?" The hot little piece of ass had landed herself in jail for prostitution and still hadn't learned her lesson.

"You must give a pretty spectacular blow job, Honey," he teased. "If you think you'll be able to work off the whole fifteen hundred." Cat smirked up at him and he knew she was going to give him some smart ass response. "You didn't learn anything from your few hours behind bars, did you Honey?"

"I'm sorry, I didn't know that having a personal epiphany was part of the deal," she sassed. "So, how about it—you game?" she asked. God help him, Repo loved his women mouthy. It was usually the type of woman he picked up at the bar, Savage Hell, and took back to his place. He found that women who hung out at the MC were always looking to hook up with a biker in hopes of becoming his ol'lady. Problem was—he had no plans of ever making any woman his for long term. He was more of a one night kind of guy. It worked for him but he was bright enough to know that if he took sexy little Cat up on her offer, he'd be out fifteen hundred and he needed that money back for his next bond.

He was always chasing the next one, hoping to find someone who fucked up big time and had no one else to call but him. He needed a big score if he planned on staying ahead of the rest of the games in town. Repo ran a respectable business and he wasn't going to run the risk of fucking that all up now over one willing woman.

"Not a chance, Honey," he breathed. "How about you just give me a real address that I'll be able to use to track you down and we can both get on with our days?" Cat had the nerve to lean into his body and pout. She smelled like sex and other men, a complete turn off for Repo. He didn't do sloppy seconds. Hell, he liked a woman who had been around and had some experience. He knew he could be a little rough with them and not worry about first times and all that bullshit. But, knowing that Cat had been on the job today, so to speak, was a complete turn off for him.

"Not going to happen, Cat," he growled.

"Well, I'm not sure what else I can offer you, Repo," she said. "I have no place to stay and in just a few hours, I'm pretty sure I'll be homeless. You have my cell, isn't that enough?" Repo ran his hand down his beard, trying to decide if he could trust Cat or not. His answer was a resounding, "Fuck no," but he had no other choice.

"Fine," he agreed. He pulled his cell from his jeans and dialed the number she had given him. Her cell phone chimed and she pulled it out of her purse.

"What are you doing?" she asked.

"I'm checking to make sure you didn't give me a bogus cell number," he admitted. She made a disgruntled noise in the back of her throat and he chuckled. "You really can't blame me, Cat. You haven't been on the up and up with me." She smiled and nodded.

"Got it," she grumbled. "You don't trust me—understood. Can I go now? I'd like to try to get a shower in before my landlord finds out that I'm home and tosses me out."

"Fine," he said. "But don't disappear Cat. You run and—" Cat held up her little hand, effectively stopping the rest of the words from coming out of his mouth.

"You'll find me," she finished for him. He watched her as she walked out of the station, sure that she was going to give him trouble. He could tell by the scared look in her eyes that she was going to run and God help him, he would do everything in his power to track her down.

What he'd do with her next was up to her, but Repo had a feeling he would like his options.

The End

To be continued in REPOssession (Savage Hell MC Book 2)

# ABOUT K.L. RAMSEY

Romance Rebel fighting for Happily Ever After!

K. L. Ramsey currently resides in West Virginia (Go Mountaineers!). In her spare time, she likes to read romance novels, go to WVU football games and attend book club (aka-drink wine) with girlfriends.

K. L. enjoys writing Contemporary Romance, Erotic Romance, and Sexy Ménage! She loves to write strong, capable women and bossy, hot as hell alphas, who fall ass over tea kettle for them. And of course, her stories always have a happy ending.

# K.L. RAMSEY'S SOCIAL MEDIA LINKS

### Facebook
https://www.facebook.com/kl.ramsey.58
**(OR)** https://www.facebook.com/k.l.ramseyauthor/

### Twitter
https://twitter.com/KLRamsey5

### Instagram
https://www.instagram.com/itsprivate2/

### Pinterest
https://www.pinterest.com/klramsey6234/

### Goodreads
https://www.goodreads.com/author/show/17733274.K_L_Ramsey

### BookBub
https://www.bookbub.com/profile/k-l-ramsey

### Amazon
https://www.amazon.com/K.L.-Ramsey/e/B0799P6JGJ/

### Ramsey's Rebels
https://www.facebook.com/groups/ramseysrebels/

### Website
https://klramsey.wixsite.com/mysite

### KL Ramsey & BE Kelly's ARC Team
https://www.facebook.com/groups/klramseyandbekellyarcteam

### KL Ramsey & BE Kelly's Street Team
https://www.facebook.com/groups/klramseyandbekellystreetteam

### Newsletter
https://mailchi.mp/4e73ed1b04b9/authorklramsey

## BE KELLY'S SOCIAL MEDIA LINKS

### Facebook
https://www.facebook.com/be.kelly.564

### Twitter
https://twitter.com/BEKelly9

### Instagram
https://www.instagram.com/bekellyparanormalromanceauthor/

### BookBub
https://www.bookbub.com/profile/be-kelly

### Amazon
https://www.amazon.com/BE-Kelly/e/B081LLD38M

### BE Kelly's Reader's group
https://www.facebook.com/groups/530529814459269/

# MORE WORKS BY K.L. RAMSEY

## The Relinquished Series
Love Times Infinity
Love's Patient Journey
Love's Design
Love's Promise

## Harvest Ridge Series
Worth the Wait
The Christmas Wedding
Line of Fire
Torn Devotion
Fighting for Justice

## Last First Kiss Series
Theirs to Keep
Theirs to Love
Theirs to Have
Theirs to Take

## Second Chance Summer Series
True North
The Wrong Mr. Right

## Ties That Bind Series
Saving Valentine
Blurred Lines
Dirty Little Secrets

K.L Ramsey

### Taken Series
Double Bossed
Double Crossed

### Owned
His Secret Submissive
His Reluctant Submissive
His Cougar Submissive (coming soon)

### Alphas in Uniform
Hellfire
His Destiny (coming soon)

### Royal Bastards MC
Savage Heat
Whiskey Tango (coming soon)

### Savage Hell MC Series
RoadKill
REPOssession (coming soon)

## WORKS BY BE KELLY (K.L.'S ALTER EGO ...)

## Reckoning MC Seer Series
Reaper
Tank
Raven

## Perdition MC Shifter Series
Ringer
Rios (coming soon)

Printed in Great Britain
by Amazon